Sex, drugs, and country music. That was the lifestyle for Emily Kendall, a Texas girl who hit it big on the country music charts—until she found herself pregnant and battling addiction. Now out of rehab and seeking a new life for herself and her unborn child, Emily returns to her hometown of McAllister. The last thing she's looking for is trouble, no matter how good it looks in uniform…

A widower, single father, and former Army Ranger struggling with PTSD, Sheriff EJ Cowley has his own demons to battle while keeping folks safe. The last thing he needs is a troubled celebrity speeding through town in her bright red Mazerati. But when someone from Emily's past threatens her safety and the peace of McAllister, EJ has no choice but to protect her. And soon both will learn there's more to the other than meets the eye. And that wounded hearts can love again…

Books by Sara Walter Ellwood

Colton Gamblers Series
Gambling On A Secret, Book One
Gambling On A Heart, Book Two
Gambling On A Dream, Book Three

Singing to the Heart
Heartstrings
Heartsong
Heartland

Published by Kensington Publishing Corporation

Heartland

A Singing to the Heart Novel

Sara Walter Ellwood

LYRICAL PRESS
Kensington Publishing Corp.
www.kensingtonbooks.com

Lyrical Press books are published by
Kensington Publishing Corp. 119 West 40th Street New York, NY 10018

All Kensington titles, imprints, and distributed lines are available at special
quantity discounts for bulk purchases for sales promotion, premiums, fund-
raising, and educational or institutional use.

To the extent that the image or images on the cover of this book depict a
person or persons, such person or persons are merely models, and are not
intended to portray any character or characters featured in the book.

Special book excerpts or customized printings can also be created to fit
specific needs. For details, write or phone the office of the Kensington
Special Sales Manager:
Kensington Publishing Corp.
119 West 40th Street
New York, NY 10018
Attn. Special Sales Department. Phone: 1-800-221-2647.

Kensington and the K logo Reg. U.S. Pat. & TM Off.
Lyrical Press and the L logo are trademarks of Kensington Publishing Corp.

First Electronic Edition: June 2016
eISBN-13: 978-1-60183-490-4
eISBN-10: 1-60183-490-X

First Print Edition: June 2016
ISBN-13: 978-1-60183-491-1
ISBN-10: 1-60183-491-8

Printed in the United States of America

To my family. Thank you for being there for me...

Chapter 1

Emily Kendall was tired of life-changing events. She'd had enough. But God or whatever fate controlled the universe wasn't done fucking with her life. "Are you sure? Hell, it's been weeks since I've even seen my husband, let alone had sex. Maybe the test was wrong."

She'd heard many life-changing words in her twenty-two years. The first had come when she was fourteen and discovered superstar country singer Seth Kendall was her biological father. A few weeks after that revelation, the man she'd grown up loving as her father had shot her real dad and planned to kidnap her to sell into sex slavery. She shuddered and rubbed her hands over the pricking of goose bumps on her bare arms.

Since then, a lot had happened. She'd become a famous country music star. Most people would even argue that she was more famous than her dad, who helped her get her first record deal when she was barely fifteen. She broke sales records set by some of the best singers in the business, won countless awards, and sponsored everything from acne creams to jeans.

When she was three months shy of turning twenty, she'd met the British pop star Fabian McPhee. They'd collaborated on a TV special for the CMT network. He was fifteen years older than her, mega famous, and super sexy. A month later while she was on tour in Australia, he'd asked her out to a nightclub.

That night had been full of firsts. Fabian introduced her to what would become her drugs of choice--cocaine and gin. Then, she'd lost her virginity to him. She'd thought she was in love. He was like no one she'd ever known. Despite her parents' outrage over their tabloid-crazed, whirlwind relationship, two months after their first date they were married by Fabian's drummer, who happened to be an ordained minister from some online course he'd taken.

The medical director of the facility sitting across the wide, gleaming oak desk leaned forward and clasped his hands. "Your blood test isn't wrong. You are pregnant."

"Fuck." She was on a birth control shot, but she'd forgotten to get it. The last time she'd seen Fabian had been about six weeks ago. They'd had sex, but she thought he'd used a condom. She couldn't remember much of the event, like most of their two years of married life together. They'd split up ten months ago, but neither of them had gotten around to filing for divorce or could resist an occasional tumble in the sack or getting high together.

Not able to sit still any longer, she stood to pace the length of the posh office and folded her arms tightly around herself to stave off the shivering. At the same time sweat ran along her hairline and down the side of her face. She'd been here for three days and already wanted to get the hell out of the medical facility. "How far along am I?"

Dr. Barton slid his finger over the screen of the computer tablet on his desk. "According to the history you gave the nurse who checked you in and your hCG level..." When she furrowed her brows trying to remember what the letters stood for, he clarified, "Pregnancy hormone. You would have to be six weeks."

She closed her eyes and took a deep breath. Her skin was too tight and hot. A coating of sweat caused her fingers to stick together, and she wiped her shaky hands on her jeans. Turning toward the window, she stared out at the woodland park surrounding the Fernwood Rehabilitation Center. In the past three years, she'd checked into the facility's drug and alcohol program to sober up three times, and each admission had been against her will. She didn't belong here because she wasn't an addict. Whose business was it if she went a little too far this last time and was booed off stage? The venue, if a college auditorium could justify that name, sucked anyway.

This news was the last thing she needed to hear. She turned and vigorously rubbed her arms, needing a hit right now. The desire for a line of coke brought to mind another issue. She remembered when her mother had been pregnant with her brother five years ago she wouldn't even take Tylenol for her headaches. Did she honestly want to know the answer to what all the coke she'd snorted could have done to her baby if her mother had been afraid to take something as harmless as over-the-counter pain pills? But she had to know if she'd harmed her child. "Do you know if the baby is okay?"

Dr. Barton stood to come around his desk. He leaned his backside on the heavy oak edge and folded his hands before him. "I don't know. Emily, there is a chance your baby will be born with problems. You are an addict." He held up his hand when she started to protest. "No, I'm not listening to your rationalizations. You've got to stop the drugs."

"I can quit. I have before."

He took a deep breath that made his shoulders rise, then fall. "And yet here you are again. Why were you admitted this time?"

She needed to get the hell away. "My manager has gotten a little too big for her pants." Maybe she should fire Trish Russell for talking her into even thinking about this place again. Trish had been her manager for three years, ever since she was promoted by her father-in-law and took Emily on as one of her first clients. She considered Trish one of her few true friends, but, sometimes, the older woman was a pain in the ass.

With a huff of derision, she spun on her heels, which made her lose her balance as dizziness whipped her world out of control. Grabbing the back of the chair to keep from falling over, she tossed over her shoulder, "I think we're done here."

"Emily, I'll let you go as soon as you tell me why you are here."

She stopped halfway to the door. If she didn't answer him, he'd only follow her. Letting out a long breath, she stared at the white-painted ceiling. "I'm here because I was too high to sing."

The past five shows were a blur. Nothing fun or amazing about any of them. No fans waiting for her to autograph their T-shirts. But then again, when had she last taken the time to talk to her fans after a show? How long had it been since she did anything special for them? Once upon a time, she'd put on massive productions in front of stadiums full to bursting with screaming, adoring fans.

Her last tour hadn't even sold out to rundown opera houses and college auditoriums. In the early days, she'd arrange spontaneous private showings for more fans than had showed up for her current tour. She'd simply leave a date, time, and place on Twitter and a hundred or more of her fans would come for a show. When had she last sent one of her own Tweets? She knew Kelly, her assistant, did all of her social media crap for her these days.

"I'm here because my record label said if I don't sober up, they're cutting me."

"They aren't happy with you?"

She shrugged and started pacing again. The temperature of the room seemed to increase with each pass across the shrinking floor space. "No.

My last album is six months past due its production deadline. But I can't help that all the songs suck."

"Why do they suck?"

Turning, she met the doctor's steady gaze. She wanted to tell Dr. Barton her label and her manager had sabotaged her by giving her shit songs, but she couldn't. Were the songs bad? Her father's old friend, pop superstar Amanda Lang, had written four of them and had given them to Emily as a gift, despite three other singers wanting them. The other two songs she'd recorded were from an award-winning songwriter, and they, too, had been sought after by the best in the business.

She blinked when the realization hit her. The songs weren't the problem nor were the studio musicians playing on the record. She was. "I don't want to talk about my career. I want to talk about my baby. Is there any way we can determine if it's okay?" As she laid her trembling hand on her belly, she silently prayed to a God she doubted would listen to anything she asked of Him. *Please let my baby be okay.*

Dr. Barton looked down at his hands, then went back to his big leather chair and sat. "I'd like you to meet with a colleague of mine. Doctor Marcella Summers is an OB/Gynecologist who specializes in babies born to addicted mothers. She'd be the person who might know the answer to your question."

She faced the wide windows again, but the early summer day and the forested mountains surrounding the center weren't what she saw. "Okay."

How was she going to handle a baby? Hell, she could barely take care of herself. What if it had a major problem from all the crap she'd put into her body?

She closed her eyes and fisted her hand over her belly. Dear God, what would Fabian say about the baby? He'd warned her when they got married he didn't want any kids. Would he blame the pregnancy on her as he had many other things over the past two years?

"Emily, I don't know an addict who easily admits they are one." Dr. Barton broke into a tirade of questions bombarding her. "By your own admission, you use cocaine at least four times a week, but most weeks you use it every day."

She glanced over her shoulder at him. He swiped his finger over his tablet, then paused to read more of her medical record. "In August twenty-eighteen, your father admitted you to Fernwood when he found you passed out on your tour bus. According to your blood toxin levels, you were only a snort of coke away from overdosing; then in June of last year, you were admitted after falling off stage and breaking your arm. Again, your blood work showed dangerous amounts of cocaine and alcohol."

Although she snickered at the memory, the humor choked in her throat, and she sobered. That had been her last stadium show. Tabloid and entertainment reporters hounded her after her release from Fernwood. Fabian's own career also took a nosedive when he was arrested for drunk driving and resisting arrest. The two of them and their antics had been a favorite topic in even mainstream news since then.

He cleared his throat and folded his hands in front of him. "Your blood results weren't as toxic this time, but if you don't make an honest attempt to get clean and stay clean, not only will you jeopardize your child, you're going to end up dead."

The truth smacked her hard in the gut. She was an addict. Up until now, she never believed she was one. She used coke and drank gin because she liked them, not because she couldn't live without them. At the reality, she curled her hand into a fist over the sour pain in her belly and admitted to herself she used drugs to deal with life and all of its shit.

Would she have become screwed up if she'd never met Fabian McPhee? Or had she been destined to a life of drug use due to her messed up childhood and sudden superstardom? Who knew? She hated the man who first introduced her to drugs and destroyed much of her life. Her country music career was dead, and the fans she'd garnered when she put out a total pop album a year and half ago at Fabian's insistence had abandoned her. She hadn't spoken to or seen her parents, except from a distance at award shows, since her marriage. Since severing her ties with her mom and dad, she hadn't seen her four-year-old brother. Now, she was responsible for developing a tiny baby who may end up paying for her lousy judgment.

She turned and met the doctor's patient brown eyes. The man had to be a saint to manage the care of spoiled brat idiots like her. "Okay, Dr. Barton. I'm an addict. I use coke because I can't deal with life." She squared her shoulders and let out a breath. "There, I owned it. Set up the appointment with the OB. But there's something else I'd like you to do." One of the conditions of admission into Fernwood was no contact with the outside world except for approved visitors on an extremely short list. "I want to file for divorce before I tell Fabian about the baby."

The doctor's surprise registered in the slightest widening of his eyes. "If that is want you want."

Emily couldn't help the snort as she sat in the chair in front of the desk again. "Oh, don't be coy, Dr. Barton. I know you've been hoping I'd ditch Fabian McPhee since the first time my father dragged my sorry ass into this place a year and a half ago." She looked at her hands as a rare moment of clarity blasted away the rosy sheen she'd painted over her life with her husband. "My counselor is right. Fabian and I do have a crazy love type of relationship. He might not beat me, but he has made me dependent on him by making me an addict."

For the first time in years, she felt relief flood over her. She smiled and met the doctor's eyes again. "For my baby and for me, I have to get away from him."

* * * *

Emily laid a t-shirt in her suitcase and turned at the knock on the doorframe. She smiled at the willowy woman as she entered the room. "I'm glad to see you. I'm ready to get out of here."

The eight weeks she'd been a resident of the rehab had been the longest time she'd ever stayed, but once she faced her demons and committed herself, she didn't want to leave until she was free of her addiction.

Trish tucked her medium-length bright red hair behind her ear. "Paul isn't happy about postponing your record," she said, referring to the CEO of Midland Records. "But I convinced him you needed a break to get completely sober and stay that way."

Emily laid another t-shirt in the case. Her reason for being at Fernwood was no secret, but the only person outside of her doctors who knew about her pregnancy was Trish. After telling her, Emily asked her to convince her record company to push her production deadline to sometime in the future. "He doesn't suspect anything, does he?"

Trish sat on the overstuffed chair in the corner of the modest room. "No. I made a convincing case about your wanting to finally quit the drugs. He's not happy, but he's also glad."

Emily moved the suitcase off to the side and sat on the edge of the bed, facing Trish. "Has Fabian signed the divorce papers?"

"Yes. Reese is filing them today, in fact." Reese Goodwin was a family friend and a Nashville divorce lawyer. "Your divorce should be final by the end of the month."

She closed her eyes and took a deep breath full of relief. Although she hadn't demanded anything of Fabian, she feared he'd delay signing the papers to end their ill-fated marriage. "Thank God."

Trish leaned back in the chair and folded her hands in her lap. "When are you going to tell him about the baby?"

With a shrug, Emily stood, opened a dresser drawer, and pulled out a stack of bras. As she set them in her bag, she said, "I'll set up a meeting with him sometime before I go home to Texas."

She planned to get out of Nashville before she started showing. At almost four months pregnant, she knew she was on borrowed time.

"How do you think he'll take the news?"

Emily went back to the drawer and took out a stack of panties. "Hopefully, he won't take the news well and will leave me and my baby the hell alone."

She swallowed at the thought of her baby never knowing her father like she hadn't known Seth, but Fabian wasn't a good man. Despite being nearly forty years old, he still partied too hard and didn't take much seriously. He'd wasted most of his own fortune and a large portion of hers on fast cars, drugs, and lavish parties. She gritted her teeth until her jaw hurt at how stupid she'd been to let him manipulate her.

"He didn't fight about selling the penthouse and the mansion?" Three months after they were married, Fabian talked her into moving out of her downtown Craftsman home she'd bought on her eighteenth birthday and into buying a twenty-million-dollar estate outside of Nashville. The place was too big and flashy and put a considerable dent into her savings. He'd convinced her by arguing that as two successful entertainers, they were expected to live in such extravagance. Besides, he swore he'd pay his share of the cost. Instead, he conned her into buying a penthouse in Manhattan. He spent a lot of time there, but she hated New York and preferred to live in Nashville.

"He wants the penthouse." Trish pulled her iPad out of her purse. The woman never went anywhere without the thing. "But he's okay with selling the Nashville property and letting you keep the money from the sale if he can keep the penthouse."

"I'm glad he wants the penthouse." Emily closed her suitcase and smiled as she turned to face Trish with her hand over the slight swell of her belly. "Because then I have a bargaining chip to keep him away from us."

Chapter 2

Today marked the second anniversary of his wife's overdose.

McAllister County, Texas, sheriff EJ Cowley hated the memory of finding Raquel in the bathtub and of their hungry six-month-old son screaming from his crib. He'd lain in his soiled diaper for at least five hours. Raquel's body had been colder than the water. Two empty medication bottles were found on the floor by the edge of the tub: one held Adderall and the other Zoloft. She had been given the latter medicine to help deal with her postpartum depression. She'd taken Adderall as a kid for ADHD, but as an adult had outgrown the need for it. He'd discovered afterward she'd bought the pills on the internet using a bank account he hadn't been aware she had. She'd become addicted to the amphetamine after the birth of their son, which formed a deadly combination with the antidepressant when taken in larger doses than a doctor would prescribe. However, the bottle of Zoloft she'd emptied hadn't been hers.

The purr of a high performance car engine broke the silence along the two-lane country road passing his driveway. He shook the memory away and focused down the long straight stretch of road heading toward town. The early morning sun glinted off the windshield of an oncoming car racing toward him.

"Damn." He hated ticketing speeders, but not because he disagreed with speeding laws. He disliked the stinking attitude most took up when they were stopped. After a night filled with cold-sweat inducing dreams interspersed with his two-year-old son's painful cries from a belly ache, the last thing he wanted to deal with was a smart-assed mouth.

When the fast cherry-red sports car passed, he clocked it at sixty miles per hour in a forty-five speed zone. Putting the portable siren he kept in his Silverado on top of the cab, he pulled out of his driveway and followed. The vehicle in front of him slowed and pulled over as he gained on it.

As he reached in the glove box for his pad of tickets, he whistled between his teeth. A Maserati with a Tennessee plate. His computer was in his official Tahoe, which was parked at the station, but he could ticket the driver and enter the citation when he got to the office. Opening the door, he picked up his hat from the side seat and put it on his head as he slid out of the pickup. He caught the female driver watching him through her side mirror and got a glimpse of dark reddish hair and big-lensed sunglasses covering most of a slender face from her reflection.

She straightened in the leather seat and smiled as he stopped at the driver's door, ducking down to look at her. Despite the sunglasses covering her green eyes, he knew her. The magazines and TV hadn't done her justice. She was one of the most beautiful women he'd ever seen. Her auburn hair was styled in a short pixie cut that seemed to make her look even more like a fairy than he'd thought of her when she was younger. A sudden flutter hit his gut and rattled his thoughts. What the hell was he nervous about? He'd met famous people before. Besides, he'd known this girl all of her life.

In spite of the reason he'd stopped her, he smiled. "Well, if it isn't Emily Ritter. Haven't seen you around here for years."

Her smile fell the moment the name *Ritter* slipped out of his mouth. "I don't go by that name any more and haven't since I was fourteen." She shot back as she glanced at his badge and the nametag above it on his uniform shirt. "Edward James Cowley." The smile returned, but this time it held a hint of mischief. She must have remembered how much he hated his full name and used it to get back at him for his flub. "You're the sheriff now? You get out of the Army?"

"I got out a little over two years ago, and yes, I'm the sheriff." EJ pushed the brim of his hat over his forehead. God, he had to focus. "The reason I stopped you wasn't to engage in small talk. You were speeding. I'll need to see your driver's license, registration, and proof of insurance."

"C'mon, since when does anyone care about speeding on this old stretch of cow path?" She removed her sunglasses to reveal eyes the color of spring grass. They'd always seemed to mesmerize him, even when she was a kid, and now wasn't any different. "Hell, the only people out here are my family, the Ritters, your family, and the Campbells."

Her voice broke the trance her beauty put him under. She definitely wasn't the girl who'd followed him around when she'd come over to the Double K to visit John Kendall, never knowing the old rancher was her grandfather.

"Actually, I own the Campbells' place. They sold the Arrowhead Ranch a year ago after Uncle Joe had a heart attack. He and Aunt Sally moved to Arizona to be closer to my mom and dad." He had to remember this woman wasn't the innocent little girl he'd teased any more. Or a stunning woman he'd like to get to know better. From what he'd heard on the radio and from the tabloid covers he'd read while standing in line at the grocery store, she'd turned into a drug addict and party hellion after marrying a British rock star. He didn't even like her music anymore, and there was a time, he'd thought she had the voice of an angel. The thought of her throwing away her talent on booze and drugs sent a spear of anger through him. Someday she'd undoubtedly end up as dead as Raquel had.

He held out his hand. "Your driver's license, Ms. Kendall."

She reached for her purse, setting on the passenger's seat, and pulled out her license, then rummaged through the glove box for her registration and insurance papers. As she handed the items to him, she smiled the sweet, breathtaking smile he'd seen splashed on magazine covers and award shows, but it never entered her hard eyes. "Fine. Here you go, Sheriff Cowley."

* * * *

Emily glared at the retreating backside of EJ Cowley as he sauntered to his SUV, but her ire at the McAllister County sheriff was soon replaced with an appreciation of the way his ass filled out the tan pants. The scrawny teenage boy who'd pulled on her pigtails and chased her around the Double K when John Kendall wasn't watching had grown up into a good-looking man.

Too bad he'd turned into a jerk.

She shook her head and rested her hand over the slight swell of her belly. Even if he was the nicest, sexiest man in the world, he was the last thing she needed. She wasn't looking for a man. Didn't want one. Her divorce had been final for almost two months, but she wouldn't ever be completely free of Fabian McPhee despite her not wanting him to be part of her child's life and his lack of paternal acknowledgement. The only way to escape him was to never let her baby know about him which she wouldn't--*couldn't*--ever do. Regardless of the pain of abandonment and the questions the knowledge of her little girl's famous father would cause her, Emily could never do to her daughter what her parents did to her. The not knowing and finding out later was worse.

Emily closed her eyes and rested her head on the seat behind her. As she rubbed over the baby growing inside her, she smiled as the memory of when she'd found out she was having a girl entered her mind.

Twelve weeks into her pregnancy, the OB/Gynecologist, Dr. Summers, performed an amniocentesis. The test results came back perfectly normal and revealed the baby's sex.

Every test the doctors performed had come back showing her baby was healthy. Dr. Summers accredited the good news to the fact Emily found out about her pregnancy early and stopped taking drugs.

"Emily... Miz Kendall? You okay?"

At the sound of EJ's deep Texas twang, she jerked her eyes open and stopped massaging her belly. No one outside of Trish Russell, Fabian, and her doctors knew about the baby, not even her parents. If he suspected her secret, he showed no signs as he held out a sheet of pink paper--her speeding ticket.

She snatched it out of his hand and tossed it on the seat beside her. "I'm fine. Tired. I've been driving for thirteen hours and want to get home to my family."

He straightened and the buttons on his uniform shirt strained across his chest as he took a deep breath. Did he lift weights? Without warning, she imagined him without the shirt and envisioned a broad chest rippling with muscle.

Irritated at the fantasy as much as by the man, she put her sunglasses back on her face and glared at him. "Are we done?"

He gave her a devilish smile, which turned his ruggedly handsome face superstar gorgeous and sent a tingle through her nervous system. "Yeah. Say hi to your mama and daddy." As she turned the key in the ignition, he tapped the top of her car. "And drive within the speed limits."

Her response was to hit the gas hard enough to send up a cloud of dust from the side of the road, but she didn't speed past forty-five. As she looked at him through her rearview mirror, she grinned at him shaking his head and standing with his arms crossed as the fine, Texas grit settled around him.

* * * *

Emily pulled into the driveway and stopped to gaze up at the wooden sign framed by a wrought iron arch over the paved tree-lined lane leading to the house her ancestors built over a hundred years ago. On the right side of the wood a bold black-painted *K* with another *K* formed from the bottom leg mimicked the brand of the seven-hundred-acre ranch. Beside the symbol, in the same bold lettering was the name: *Double K Ranch*. Below that read, *Seth and Abigail Kendall, Owners*. Despite having the four years she'd lived in the large Victorian house broken up by staying in Nashville with her dad or being on tour with him, she considered this place home.

A sensation of fluttering in her lower belly had her gasping as it did every time she experienced it. With a racing heart, she glanced down as she pressed both palms over her baggy t-shirt and held her breath. When the movement tickled her insides again, almost as if a butterfly was caught beneath her skin, she exhaled and laughed.

"You're happy to be home too, aren't you, baby girl?" She sat there for a long time waiting for the quickening again, but nothing happened. "Okay, maybe you're as nervous as I am."

She had no idea what to expect from her parents. Although, they'd voiced their worry and disapproval of her marriage to Fabian, they had never pushed her away. If anything, at first, her dad had tried to keep her close. But after he'd found her unconscious on her tour bus and had her admitted into Fernwood, she refused to speak to her mother or father again. Fabian had fueled her anger by accusing her parents of wanting to control her life.

Oh, how wrong she had been.

With a sigh, she stared into the distance at the large white house with its dark green shutters and gingerbread trim, then turned the key in the ignition. "Well, baby girl, let's go and admit they were right."

She parked the car to the side of the three-car semi-detached garage and got out. As she stretched her back, she looked around at the old familiar buildings. The barn across the lane from the house must have been recently painted and a new stable and training facility had been built in the middle of a pasture she used to ride through. Her mother had mentioned a few years ago she'd like to try her hand at raising and training horses. She must have decided to go for it.

With a deep breath, Emily headed toward the house.

"Emily?"

At the sound of her father's deep voice, she turned toward the man standing at the open barn door. "Hi, Daddy."

Her childhood idol stared back at her as if she was a mirage. Wearing a beat-up tan Stetson, faded jeans, scuffed boots, and a plaid western shirt with the sleeves rolled up to his elbows, he looked more like a ranch hand then a famous superstar country singer. Her heart stuttered over a few beats as both love and admiration filled her. She may not have known Seth Kendall was her father as a little girl, but he'd more than stepped up to fill the job during her teenage years, even making her dreams come true.

Dreams she destroyed with drugs and hard living.

She swallowed as the silence stretched. Maybe she shouldn't have come home. "I hope you don't mind me being here."

He ran across the wide driveway, and before Emily could process what was happening, he wrapped her up in a tight bear hug which she returned with equal fervor.

"This is your home." He placed a kiss on her forehead and held her far enough away to meet her gaze. She was shocked to see a tear form at the corner of one of his bright green eyes, the same shape and color as her own. "You're always welcome here, sunshine."

At the use of the nickname he'd given her when they'd first met, she wrapped her arms around him and let the relief flood over her as she rested her cheek on his chest. The spiced sandalwood scent of him surrounded her, comforting and forgiving, and she closed her eyes as tears stung her sinuses. She feared if she started crying, she wouldn't ever stop. "I'm sorry, Daddy. For everything. I've made such a mess of my life."

He rubbed her back and rested his chin on her head, like he'd done since they'd first met eight years ago. At times like this, she wished she'd known him all her life. Mike Ritter--the man she'd believed to be her father until she met Seth--and she had been close, but they'd never had the relationship she and Seth shared.

"The important thing is you're here now." His deep voice trembled as if he was holding in a massive wave of emotion. He swallowed and slowly stepped back, but didn't completely let her go as he wrapped his arm around her shoulders. "C'mon. Let's go find your mother."

She sniffed and wiped at the stray tears on her cheeks with the back of her hand. "Is Johnny home?"

He squeezed her shoulders and his smile beamed as bright as the morning sun. "You just missed him. Your momma took him to preschool. He'll be home in a few hours." He stopped at the steps leading to the wraparound porch. "You're going to make the kid's day when he gets home. He idolizes you."

She shook her head. "He shouldn't. I'm one messed up woman these days."

Dad brushed at a stray strand of her hair lying on her forehead. "No. You're a strong woman trying to get her life back on track. I knew you were on your way to healing when I heard about the divorce and that you were in rehab for longer than a week."

She glanced away. The hope in his voice nearly broke down the damn holding back her tears.

Chapter 3

EJ was logging into his computer when the office door he'd left ajar opened. He looked up and swallowed a curse. Dealing with his brother-in-law today wasn't at the top of his to-do list.

Trevor Marshall stood in the middle of his office. Dressed in a pair of black designer slacks and a pale pink dress shirt that matched the wine, pink, and black tie, the metrosexual law student looked as out of place in the ranch town of McAllister as a pile of cow shit on Fifth Avenue.

"Mama wanted to know if you were coming over to dinner tonight. She'd like to see Austin," Trevor said, referring to EJ's two year old son.

EJ sat back in his chair and folded his arms over his chest. He didn't understand Glenda's insistence of having a memorial dinner for Raquel every year to remember her life. None of them needed reminding she was dead. He'd made the mistake of attending last year and had to leave early. His memories made the day depressing enough; he didn't need to sit around looking at photo albums and telling stories of what an angel Raquel had been. He'd loved his wife--once--but she had never worn a halo. "Tell her I have other plans."

Trevor narrowed his brown eyes. "What about Austin?"

EJ shrugged. "I'll bring him over this weekend. But tonight, we have plans."

If eating the leftover pot roast his brother's wife had given him, watching the Rangers game, and drinking a beer or two after he put the baby to bed at eight o'clock justified as plans.

"What's more important than family?"

His brother-in-law's tenacity matched that of the Marshall's bulldog when he was on one of his mother's errands. Glenda had babied her only son as if he was a crown prince, and although, Trevor was twenty-three years old, he'd never let go of his mother's skirt. "I never said family wasn't important, but frankly, I'm not interested in revisiting the picture-perfect life your mother insists on painting for Raquel."

Trevor's eyes widened as he gasped. "How dare you say such a thing today?"

EJ had enough. He stood and leaned over his desk. "Look. I loved your sister, but life with her had never been perfect for me. She thought she was a princess, and I'll admit at first I treated her like one, but she was lazy, demanding and at times a down-right bitch on wheels." This time Trevor's face paled and he thinned his lips. EJ didn't care that everything he said would, no doubt, be relayed to the queen of bitchdom, his mother-in-law. He was on a roll. "The last straw for me was when we brought our baby home from the hospital and she refused to even look at him."

"She was depressed!"

"I get that." And he did, kind of. The doctor explained her postpartum depression was caused by her hormones returning to normal more quickly than she could become accustomed to and a predisposition to depression. But he knew it went deeper. She'd hated being pregnant, despite having a trouble-free time and an easy delivery. He'd caught her staring in their bedroom mirror when she was about eight months and telling their baby how much she hated him for making her fat and ugly. The memory sent a stab of pain into his heart. How could a mother hate her own baby, a child she'd created with a man she'd claimed to love? Sure, the pregnancy hadn't been planned, and wasn't at the ideal time in their renewed relationship, but he thought she wanted a family. Until she got pregnant. Had she suffered from postpartum depression, or was she depressed because now she had a baby she'd despise taking care of? Or was she angry because she married him because she was pregnant? After all, they had sex the first night they were together after a long breakup. Maybe she'd never intended to have a future with him.

He kept those thoughts to himself. "But instead of seeking help, she refused and started using drugs."

He stopped before he went any further. Before he admitted he'd dealt with depression, too, but couldn't understand why Raquel killed herself. No one knew the bottle of Zoloft she'd emptied belonged to him. He'd never taken more than three of the antidepressant pills the VA doctor prescribed for him to help with the PTSD he developed after a mission he'd commanded had gone terribly wrong. As he sat in his leather chair, he buried the memory of the five soldiers, who lost their lives under his leadership, and the dead American ambassador and her advisor he'd been sent to save in the back of his mind.

He reached for the speeding ticket he'd written that morning lying on the corner of his desk. "Now if you will excuse me, I have work to do."

Trevor glanced at the ticket and wrinkled his brow. "Emily Kendall? Is she back in town?"

Not liking his brother-in-law's tone, he leaned back in the chair and studied him, leaving the ticket on the desk. "Yeah. Guess after her last stay at Betty Ford or whatever posh spa rehab and her divorce, she came home." A memory wiggled to the surface and a surge of irritation not unlike jealousy, which made no sense, scalded his blood stream. "You dated her in high school."

Trevor stared at the ticket. "No, we never dated. We were nothing but friends. Mama hated her. Said Emily would ruin me. Then she got the record deal and we drifted apart." He met EJ's gaze. "How'd she look?"

Like sex in designer sunglasses.

Where the hell did that come from?

EJ distracted himself by shrugging and picking up the ticket. "I guess okay. At least she didn't look stoned like she did last fall on the *CMA Awards*."

"Hopefully she'll clean herself up now that she's gotten rid of the rock star." Trevor shifted his feet and looked down at his shiny manicured fingernails--did he polish the things?--with a pinched expression.

Had his suspicions about his brother-in-law's sexual orientation been wrong? Trevor was a decent-looking guy, but as far as EJ knew, he'd never had a girlfriend. Was the reason not because he was gay, but because he was pining after Emily Kendall?

Trevor seemed to shake himself and looked up at EJ. "I guess I can't convince you to come to dinner tonight."

"No. Now get out of here. I have a job to do."

Trevor nodded and left, but EJ stared at the ticket in his hand. Why did he find Emily Kendall damned intriguing?

He crumbled the ticket and tossed it into the trash. Guess now, he'd have to make sure he bumped into her to let her know he'd lost the ticket before he had a chance to report it to the DMV.

* * * *

Emily struggled to not cry and concentrated on the death grip with which she hugged the cup of tea her mother had brewed for her after their tearful reunion. As she had done when she'd met her father outside, Emily fought the deluge she was holding behind a flimsy thread of self-control, but a few drops slipped by. She sipped the tea sweetened with pasteurized organic honey and savored the flavor. She'd drunk diet crap for such a long time she forgot how much she loved the slight tangy sweetness of honey in her favorite hot beverage.

Her mother sat across the table and wiped at her eyes with a paper napkin. Her long, black braid rested over her right shoulder. Momma's hair had never been that dark. Had she started dyeing it? The thought that her mother might be going gray made her throat constrict. The tan complexion Momma had inherited from her Native American mother was darker than Emily had recalled it being. She must be working outside more now that she'd taken on raising horses in addition to overseeing the management of the ranch. She may have turned forty years old in January, but she was still as beautiful as Emily remembered.

Her father sat two cups of coffee on the table, then claimed the chair beside Momma. Without his hat, Emily noticed the traces of gray in his strawberry hair at his temples. He'd shaved off the goatee he'd sported for most of his twenty-two-year music career to hide the long jagged scar on his chin. Without the facial hair, he looked even more handsome than he had as a younger man; especially with the crinkles at the corners of his jade eyes, making him look distinguished as well.

His forty-first birthday was coming up on the twenty-fifth--a week away. She wanted to ask if her parents had anything planned, but before she had a chance her mother picked up her mug and asked, "How far along are you?"

Emily choked as she swallowed her tea. After sputtering for a few seconds, she smiled. "I should've known I couldn't keep it a secret for too long with you."

Dad drew his brows together and looked between her and Momma. "Well, I'm as much in the dark as a burned-out light bulb. Would y'all like to enlighten me?"

Momma grinned and patted his arm. "Emily?"

She took a deep breath and let it out slowly. Exhaustion from driving all night weighed her down now that some of the tension of the reunion was over. "I'm pregnant."

She smiled at the way her father's eyes widened. Then a grin spread over his face. "Damn…" She couldn't help the chuckle at the utter awe in Dad's voice. "I'm going to be a granddaddy?"

Momma laughed and leaned in to kiss his cheek, then she met Emily's gaze again. "Now answer my original question."

"I'm twenty-six weeks." She suspected her mother was concerned about what the drugs she'd taken might have done to the baby. "I found out when I was admitted to Fernwood." She told them about the conversation she'd had with Dr. Barton. When her mother asked about the baby's health, she assured her that Dr. Summers did several tests to determine that she was carrying a healthy baby girl.

"A girl, eh?" Dad sat back in his seat, a grin tugging at his lips.

"I thought about keeping the sex a secret, but figured somewhere I'd let it slip anyway." She rested her hands over her belly. "I think of her as my baby girl."

"You never were any good at keeping secrets." Her mother let a cautious smile slip into her otherwise pensive expression.

Shaking her head, Emily lifted her cooled tea to take a sip. "I know you're both wondering what Fabian thinks about the baby."

Her father shrugged and leaned over his arms. "I figured you'd get around to it. How long do you think you'll be staying?"

She set her cup onto the table and stared into it. "I'd like to make my home here. There's nothing for me in Nashville."

"You're leaving music?" Her mother's surprise had Emily looking up.

"I haven't decided yet… But if I do go back, I need to remember why I wanted to be a singer in the first place. I need to find my roots. Where better to do that than here in the heartland." She glanced around the massive custom kitchen her father had built onto the house after buying it when her grandfather died. The whitewashed cabinets with their sand-colored granite countertops, the large windows overlooking the backyard pool, and the acres of pastures dotted with cattle beyond filled the spaces where homesickness swamped her. However, it wasn't missing her family and her home that caused the restlessness. She missed the music she grew up listening to.

She met her parents' expectant gazes. "Right now, my main goal is to raise my baby."

"I hate to ask, but…is Fabian the father? I thought you were separated." Momma's brows beetled.

"Unfortunately, yes, he's her father." Emily snorted and finished her tea. "We were separated when I got pregnant." She looked into her cup and considered her words, and decided to be brutally honest. "But we liked getting high together and we liked…" God, how do you tell your parents you like sex? Honesty was greatly overrated at that moment.

"Sex?" Momma provided.

Her father let out a breath that may have been a gasp of pain. "Abby… Geez, I got the picture without you narrating it."

Nodding, heat rushed to her face, but she trudged on by answering her mother's question. No way could she look at her father. "He wants nothing to do with the baby. He never wanted kids. Knowing how he felt, I wanted to be free of him as soon as I found out I was pregnant. Not only because he helped me destroy my life--my career--but for the baby. Reese Goodwin expedited my divorce. Fabian agreed to sell the Nashville mansion, but wanted the Manhattan penthouse."

She shrugged, remembering the confrontation she had with Fabian yesterday when she'd stopped by his hotel to tell him about the pregnancy. "When I told him about the baby, he raged like a banshee that I'd gotten pregnant on purpose. I simply told him he'd never have to see either one of us again. I think he eventually realized I could have fought for child support during our divorce, but didn't. Instead, I cut all ties, besides giving him the penthouse, I signed over the rights to the songs we'd written together, both the ones recorded and the few that haven't been published yet. I don't want my name professionally connected to his."

She sighed and it turned into a yawn.

"Did you drive all night?" Dad asked.

She nodded. "Yeah. I'd packed everything up, and then met Fabian at the Marriot yesterday afternoon. After telling him about the baby, I left and headed home." The jerk had thought she'd wanted to meet with him for drugs and sex despite them now being divorced--until she pushed away his advances to drop her baby bomb.

Her mother stood. "Let me get your room ready." She turned to Dad. "Why don't you bring in her things?"

"Of course." He followed to his feet. "You couldn't have gotten much in that car."

She shook her head, and with a tired breath, she stood to lead her father out to the driveway. "No. Gabe is bringing the rest of my stuff. He should be here by the weekend."

"Gabe?" Dad paused at the door. Gabe McKenna was her father's best friend, and she'd long ago started thinking of the fellow country singer as an uncle.

"When Trish told me he was in town laying down the last tracks for his next record, I gave him a call." Her manager had once been Gabe's personal assistant before she became a talent manager with her father-in-law's firm. The two of them were still good friends. "He was more than willing to drive a rented van back to Texas. I think he was thrilled I was finally getting my head screwed on straight."

Dad wrapped his arm around her shoulders and pulled her close after they stepped onto the porch. "You could have called me."

"I could have. But Gabe had long ago told me if I needed anything, to call him. Besides, I wanted to surprise you and Momma. I think Gabe wants to talk to you about something."

Before she'd left to tell Fabian about the baby, she'd took her last walk through the mansion she'd listed the day after getting out of rehab. She'd contracted a consignment company to sell the furniture after the sale of the estate. Everything else she'd given to charity. Packing up what she'd wanted to bring with her to Texas surprisingly hadn't taken long.

Her father hefted the suitcase from the trunk of the car. The rest of her stuff, which consisted of some of her other clothes, her favorite guitars, a banjo she'd taught herself how to play, and all of her awards, were in the van she rented for Gabe to drive to the ranch on his way home in Bluebonnet Creek in Brown County. The trip was out of his way, but he'd refused to accept any payment and seemed more than happy to take on the burden.

"Gabe is trying to convince me to go in with him and form our own record label." Her father closed her trunk.

"Are you thinking about it?"

As they headed up the walkway to the porch, he said, "I am, but there's a lot at stake. We'll have to put a lot of capital into the venture I'm not sure either of us have."

"I think it's a great opportunity. Look what Show Dog Records has done for Toby's career."

"I know there's money to be made. Thing is I'd hate to leave Midland Records. I've been there since they first signed me twenty-two years ago. Paul Calabrese has been good to me and signed a lot of the acts I've brought to him. Like you and Gabe," he said, referring to the president of Midland and another close friend. Paul's friendship with her father was what probably saved her ass from being dropped like poop from a flock of pigeons when Trish asked for an indefinite extension on her production deadline for her current record.

He opened the screen door into the kitchen. "I also know where Gabe's coming from. We're both getting old."

She moved into the kitchen and shook her head. "You're still making number one records. Gabe is too."

"True. But there will come a time when we'll stop selling out stadiums and stop racing up the charts. There's a lot of young, hot talent out there." Grinning, he looked over his shoulder at her as they headed down the hall to the stairs. "I know what it's like to be upstaged by my opening act. I don't want that to happen again."

She laughed because she'd been that opening act. "What can I say? Sorry I stole your fans."

At the painful thought that none of those fans were hers anymore, she lost the smile. People still wanted her autograph, and she couldn't go anywhere without someone noticing her and making a fuss, but most of her earlier supporters had deserted her. The groupies and media following her now simply wanted a piece of her because she was famous.

Swallowing, she turned to him at the open door of her old bedroom. "Dad, I think you'd make a wonderful music executive. You have a great ear for talent and you care about what people want to hear."

He set her case inside her room, then drew her into his arms and kissed her forehead. "I love you, sunshine."

"I love you, too, Daddy." She had to swallow the lump forming in her throat as the tears she'd been holding in came rushing back.

Her mother finished fluffing her pillows and moved in beside them. She took Emily into her arms after Dad stepped away, hugging her close and hoarsely whispering in her ear, "I'm happy you came home. I love you and I'm proud of you."

"I love you." She clung to her mother. The torrent of tears was too much, and they gushed from her hot and utterly liberating. Why had she held them back?

Her father wrapped his arms around both her and Momma and held them as she cried until there was nothing left. Emily slowly moved away from them and had never felt freer.

She was home.

Now, she could truly heal.

Chapter 4

After showering in her en suite bathroom, Emily dressed in a pair of jean shorts she couldn't button anymore and a baggy sleeveless shirt. As she looked at herself in the full-length mirror on her closet door, she tied a knot in the bottom of the shirt, hoping to make the thing look less sack-like, without giving away her belly's distinctive curve. She fussed with the slack in the material until she was satisfied with the result.

Hiding the pregnancy was getting harder and harder, but she wasn't ready to go public. What if she couldn't take the criticisms she knew would be waiting for her when the world learned her secret? Although she probably deserved the ugliness sure to follow her reveal, she didn't need more people telling her she was a fucking idiot. She was good at that all by herself.

Giving up the battle with her flyaway short hair, she set her brush on dresser and stuck her tongue out at her still groggy reflection, then headed out to face the world--and to find something to eat. Her last meal had been a fast food burger and a chocolate milkshake she'd bought in a truck stop outside Oklahoma City.

She opened the door of her bedroom and stopped dead. Her baby brother sat on the carpeted floor of the hallway. His legs crossed as he pretended to be flying a plane, which at closer inspection proved to be an X-wing fighter from *Star Wars*, and held a toy lightsaber in his right hand. He looked up with large hazel eyes, dropped the fighter, and scrambled to his feet. "Sissy! Momma said you came home, but I didn't beweeve her."

He had the same trouble with *L*s she'd had as a little kid. She still remembered telling people her name was "Emiwee." With a smile, she knelt down before the four-year-old. "Now, has Momma ever lied to you?"

He shook a curly head of four-alarm fire red hair and a big smile spread across a face scattered with freckles. She'd seen pictures of her dad when he was little and Johnny looked so much like him it was downright scary.

It was as if he'd been cloned and none of her mother's genetics had been consulted. But then, Emily didn't have much of their mother in her either. She was a dead ringer for her long dead great-grandmother. In fact, the resemblance to the woman had clued her grandfather, John Kendall, in that she was Seth's daughter and didn't belong to Mike Ritter when she was a little girl.

Then you're lucky.

She understood why her mother lied concerning her paternity. After Mike Ritter's trial, she discovered the depth of his depravity and of his manipulation of Momma and Seth. However, at the end of the day, she regretted missing out a whole childhood with her real father.

Glad her baby brother would never have his world turned upside down as she had, she reached over and ruffled Johnny's hair. "How long have you been waiting out here in the hall?"

He shrugged his small shoulders and studied his green lightsaber. "I dunno. Since I got home."

She glanced at her phone, then slid it into her back pocket. It was now five o'clock. She'd been asleep for over six hours. Pre-school couldn't be more than two or three hours long. Had he been sitting here waiting for her to wake up for hours? The implication humbled her and terrified her. Her father had mentioned Johnny idolized her, but she didn't want the devotion. She didn't deserve it.

He held up the extended plastic collapsible sword. "I'm a Jedi Knight."

"I see. You like *Star Wars*?"

His nod sent his curls bouncing. "Yep. I saw aw the movies." He scrunched up his face into a scowl and brandished the lightsaber in a wide arc, as he made a swishing sound between his teeth. "I reawy don't wike the Sith."

What would her little brother do if she told him she'd dated one of the actors from the new movies a few years ago? She laughed and stood. "Me either. I've seen all the movies, too." Her stomach took that moment to let out a loud growl.

His eyes widened again and he pointed to her midsection with the toy sword. "You have a wion in there!"

Chuckling, she curled her hands into claws and growled. "An alien lion. She's hungry and likes to eat Jedi. Let's go down and find something to feed her, or she'll come out and eat you."

He let out a squeal of delight and ran toward the stairs. "Momma! Momma! Emiwee has a wion in her bewee and she's gonna eat me!"

Her mother's roast beef, mashed potatoes, and sweet corn from her garden were some of the most delicious food she'd eaten in months, maybe years. She enjoyed the fun welcoming warmth of her family, the nonstop questions of her baby brother, and she ate more than she should have. Afterward, Emily started gathering dishes, but her mother stopped her when she said, "There is someone who I think would love to see you."

Emily frowned, who on the ranch would want to see her? Maybe the ranch's two foremen, Tucker and Vince Cowley, cared enough about her to visit. The Cowleys had lived and worked on the Double K since their father had been her grandfather's foreman. Despite knowing the family since she was little, she'd never been close to any of them. Unless she counted her relationship with the clan's youngest member. At the thought of EJ Cowley, a thrill slithered through her and settled deep in her belly. Could he have come over to see her as the friend he'd been when they were kids and not as the pain-in-the-ass, ticket-happy sheriff?

"Who?" she asked and shook away the unwanted wish.

Her father took a rinsed plate from Momma and set in the dishwasher rack. "I can't believe you didn't want to see her as soon as you got here. There was a time I swore you loved that horse more than people."

At the reference to a horse, she knew instantly who she needed to visit. "Tinkerbell!" She huffed and shook her head. "God, how could I be this dense?"

Because you were thinking of a certain hot sheriff instead of one of the best friends you've ever had.

With the berating running through her mind, she grabbed a bag of baby carrots from the fridge and an apple from the bowl on the counter. Her father's voice behind her told her where to find the horse she'd had since she was six years old. With the screen door banging closed behind her, she jogged across the driveway to the corral next the barn.

She opened the gate and slipped inside. The ten horses lifted their heads from the grass they were munching to look at her. A pinto mare and bay gelding belonging to her mother before her marriage to Seth were the first to recognize her and walk over. Both horses had gray in their muzzles, and the bay had a slight limp, likely from arthritis. Despite being too old to ride anymore, they seemed to be enjoying their retirement. A third horse watched the older horses. She wasn't as old as the others in the pasture, but she was almost twenty. The mare whinnied and flicked her ears forward to listen to Emily's voice as she murmured to the horses eating baby carrots from her palm.

Mike Ritter had given the sorrel to her as a sixth birthday gift and she named the mare Tinkerbell, after her favorite Disney character. She must have been jealous of the attention Emily was giving Jack and Lacy because she pushed the pinto and trotted over to her.

"Hey... You never were this rude?" Emily smiled at Tinkerbell. She and the horse had been inseparable growing up.

Lacy ate the last of the carrots, then she and Jack moved aside to let Tinkerbell get closer to her mistress. The thoroughbred had been trained to barrel race, and Emily had taken to the sport not long after Mike had given the mare to her. After his trial for shooting Seth, attempted kidnapping of her, and the rest of his grocery list of crimes, she'd wondered if he'd given her the horse to distract her from her dream of becoming a singer. He'd been paranoid someone would recognize either her as Seth's daughter due to her talent, or by her resemblance to him, which singing made more pronounced.

Tinkerbell whinnied bringing her back to the present. "Okay, I brought you a snack, too. Hold your horses." She grinned at the old phrasing she'd used as a kid and tucked the empty plastic bag into her pocket, then held out the apple she'd snagged.

The mare nickered and sniffed at the offering before taking a bite. Emily stepped in beside the horse and stroked her sleek neck. "God, I've missed you, Tink. Life was much simpler back then."

Tinkerbell finished her snack and nodded her head as if she agreed with Emily, and she laughed as she hugged the mare. "You're in here with the old folks, eh? When was the last time anyone rode you?"

Emily considered saddling her up and taking her out, but almost as soon as the thought entered her mind she rejected it. She hadn't been on a horse for over three years. Not that she'd forgotten how to ride, nor did she distrust Tinkerbell, but she didn't have any riding clothes or boots. She stepped in front of the horse and stroked over the long white blaze down Tink's face.

"I'm sorry, but I can't ride you right now." She kissed the horse above her nose, and Tink nuzzled her cheek. "We'll go out tomorrow. How about that?"

"I remember when you rode that horse everywhere you went."

Startled by the deep voice, she turned. EJ Cowley leaned on the top rail of the fence, and from the look of it, he'd been there for a while. He'd changed out of the brown uniform of the McAllister County sheriff's department. She couldn't help looking him over. Dressed in worn boots, faded jeans, a blue western shirt, and a brown Stetson, he epitomized every sexy cliché existing about how a cowboy should look.

Her heart sped up at the way those clothes fit him. Which irritated the hell out of her. She turned back to her horse and stroked her long face. "What are you doing here?"

"My sister-in-law watches my son while I'm at work."

She stilled. Had she been quasi-lusting after a married man? Hadn't he married Raquel Marshall? She glanced over her shoulder at his left hand. No ring. But then a lot of cowboys didn't wear their wedding bands when they were working. The risk of getting it caught on something was too great.

Despite his clothes, he must have come off duty as the county's ticket-happy sheriff not too long ago. She patted Tink's shoulder. "See you in the morning, girl." As she headed toward the man, who was not hiding the fact he appreciated what he saw, she guessed he wasn't still married, but she'd been around the world a few times and knew not to take a man's blatant interest as proof of anything. "You have a son. How is Raquel these days?"

She was close enough to notice his gray eyes had turned as haunted as a gravestone when she asked about his wife. He looked to the left, toward his brother's house, and from the way a muscle twitched in his jaw, he must have gritted his teeth. "She committed suicide two years ago today."

"Oh... I'm sorry. I didn't know." She stammered. What else had happened to the people she'd once considered friends she was unaware of? "How old is your little boy?"

He took a deep breath and met her gaze again. She studied his eyes as they moved over her face. God, he had the most fascinating eyes. They weren't truly blue, but the gray was an odd shade. Too light to be slate, but too dark to be silver. They reminded her of her great-grandmother's pewter candleholders.

"Two."

As silence engulfed them, she turned to head for the gate. She had no idea what was up with the sheriff, and she didn't like her desire to ask. EJ Cowley may have filled her schoolgirl fantasies, but she wasn't the wide-eyed kid who crushed after the local cowboy-turned-soldier.

"Emwee?"

At the sound of her name, she glanced past EJ to the porch. Johnny stood there with his toy lightsaber and x-wing. She promised to play a video game with her brother. "Well, it was good seeing you again, EJ."

She was halfway across the drive when his voice stopped her. "By the way"--He cleared his throat--"I lost your ticket..."

Stopping in the middle of the driveway, she looked over her shoulder at him. His face puckered as if he'd eaten a lemon soaked in vinegar. He took his hat off and ran a hand through his short hair. The setting sun turned the tresses a gleaming gold.

"You lost it?" Damned if she'd make it easy on him. "After going through all the trouble of stopping me a mile away from home?"

Setting his hat back on his head, he cleared his throat again and stood with his feet apart. He gave a quick jerk with his head in the affirmative. "Can't find it anywhere. No ticket. No proof. You're off the hook."

Holy crap, he was gorgeous, and heat flooded her to pool in her belly. She turned, not wanting him to see the way he affected her, and headed for the porch, then lied through her teeth. "Good, because I've already tossed it." She had every intention of paying the fine, but she was glad he *lost* the ticket. No decent cop would lose a ticket. Maybe he did it out of remembrance of their childhood friendship. Or was he as attracted to her as she was to him?

With an inward shake of herself, she didn't let a possible answer formulate in her muddled brain. She couldn't be anything to him. *You're pregnant with another man's child and don't need the added stress!* At the door into the kitchen, she ruffled Johnny's hair and turned, ignoring her self-admonishment. "See you around, EJ."

"Yeah... See you around." He tipped his hat and turned on his heel to amble toward his extended cab Silverado.

From inside the screen door, she watched the way he filled out the backside of his Wrangler's and muttered, "Hell yeah, I hope so."

Chapter 5

What the hell happened?

EJ hadn't acted that damned tongue tied around a girl since he asked Raquel to the eighth grade dance. The screen door slapped closed after Emily entered the kitchen. With the vision of her long bare legs replaying in his mind, he turned on his heel and headed for his truck. He'd always thought she had a great pair of legs when he'd seen her splashed across the magazines or on TV, but seeing them up close and personal was enough to remind him how long it had been since he'd been with a woman.

When Raquel and he were married for a month, he'd been called up for a special mission with his Army Ranger unit. She was three months pregnant. By the time he'd come back from the mission that ended his military career two months later, she refused to sleep with him, claiming she was too uncomfortable from the pregnancy and he was too moody all the time to have sex. After the birth, they barely looked at each other and he suffered from horrible nightmares. He remained sleeping on the futon in the living room of their two-bedroom apartment.

Closing his eyes, he waited for the pain to hit over losing Raquel, but nothing filled his heart but anger. After his run-in with his brother-in-law, he couldn't stop thinking about his relationship with his wife. They started dating their freshman year of high school, then continued while they went to college at Texas A & M. She'd studied art, while he double majored in ranch management and criminal justice. He'd joined the ROTC to help pay for school and decided to make a career out of the military. Raquel hated his decision, especially when graduation came around and he sat at the top of his class in both majors. He could have had his choice of civilian jobs, but chose to join Military Intelligence with the rank of second lieutenant. After two years, he joined the Army Rangers with the hope of someday qualifying for Special Forces.

Raquel and he had broken up for about four years after graduation. He went off to the Middle East at the height of the ISIS Crisis while she dated every available bachelor in McAllister County. After his second deployment four years ago, he'd come home for Christmas, and before he knew what happened, they were engaged. They'd married a month after she announced she was pregnant, then a month later he was called into service to help rescue two American dignitaries who'd been kidnapped by terrorists.

With a punch at the steering wheel, he stopped the memories. If any of his past caused pain, it was the memory of the mission that had gone south and his bad decisions that had led to the deaths of most of his team and the two civilians he'd been sent to protect.

He pulled into the driveway of his brother's home, the same house he grew up in. The Kendalls had deeded the manager's house and three-hundred acres to Vince not long after Abby and Seth married. They also gave his oldest brother the neighboring three-hundred-acre ranch and house Abby had brought into the marriage. He glanced back at the large white Victorian in the distance. A half mile separated the main ranch house and Vince's home, but the distance may have been from him to the moon, regardless of whether the Kendalls treated the Cowleys like family or not.

Sniffing after a woman like Emily Ritter or Kendall or whatever the hell she called herself would prove his idiocy. She was out of his league, and too much like Raquel. Emily would be the same kind of woman who loved excess and easily depressed when she didn't get her way.

Why was he attracted to her if he truly believed this? How could he forget his own principles and destroy a speeding ticket for nothing more than a chance to see her again?

Was he that hard up for a tumble between the sheets?

If anyone ever found out what he'd done with the ticket, it would add fuel to the fire of mistrust he already lived with. Mike Ritter's misuse of the office of sheriff had tarnished it in the minds of the county's people. He'd not been the first sheriff elected after Ritter's arrest and imprisonment, but he had a long way before he gained the people's trust.

As he crossed the wide front porch, he shook the unpleasant thoughts from his mind and opened the screen door into his childhood home. The scent of tomato sauce and garlic bread enticed his nose and the high-pitched sounds of kids playing in the room to the right assaulted his hearing when he stepped into the small entry.

"We need to move the herd out of the east pasture," his oldest brother, Tucker, was saying to Vince as EJ removed his hat and hung it onto the hook by the door. "The grass in there is getting too thin to support that many head."

From the living room, Vince noticed EJ at the doorway over their brother's shoulder and nodded toward him, then said in response to Tucker, "Fine by me. Have you asked the boss about it?"

Tucker tipped his bottle of Coors and took a long drink. "We have a meeting with her in the morning to talk about it." He turned toward EJ and held up his bottle as a wide grin spread across his sunburned face. Of the five Cowley kids, Tucker looked the most like their dad with his dark hair and eyes. "Hey, little brother, where the heck did you go?"

Tucker had been following EJ onto the ranch, but he'd stopped when he noticed Emily in the corral with the horses. Damn, Tucker would never let his need to see Emily go.

Despite Tucker and Vince being twelve and ten years his senior respectively, they were as close as any three brothers could be, and always had been. They also had two sisters. Lori taught seventh grade and lived over the state line in Oklahoma, and Becky worked as an accountant over in Amarillo. Both of them were closer to EJ in age, but they may have been strangers, and at times like this, he wished his older brothers didn't know him so well. They would never let him live down his stupid schoolboy fascination with McAllister's pop star princess.

"Sheriff's business, that's all." EJ shrugged and pointed to Vince's beer bottle. "You have another one of those, or has he"--he jerked his thumb toward Tucker--"drunk it all?"

"Sheriff's business, eh?" Tucker crinkled his brow and lifted his beer to his lips, but before taking a sip, he asked, "With who?" Before EJ could answer, Tucker lowered the bottle and lost the puzzled pucker, then laughed and slapped him on the shoulder. "Holy hell, you aren't sniffing after Emily Kendall, are you? I saw her in the pasture with her horse."

"No, of course not." EJ snatched the opened beer from Vince the moment he reentered the living room from the kitchen, and took a long pull on the bottle. He couldn't confess his reason for stopping at the big house.

"What'd I miss?" Vince looked from Tucker to EJ.

With a smirk, Tucker pointed his bottle at EJ. "I think our little brother hasn't gotten over his crush on Emily."

EJ choked as he swallowed the cold beer. "What the fuck?" He swiped the back of his hand over his mouth. "She's like eight years younger than me. I never had a crush on her. God, she was a little girl when I went to college and joined the Army. What do you think I am? A pedophile? She was like ten, and I was eighteen!"

But she's all woman now. The memory of her long lean body, which had enough curves all in the right places to be sexy, flashed through his mind. His face flushed hot, and he knew he'd played right into Tucker's hands.

His brothers laughed, and Tucker patted him on the back. "Yeah, well, she sure isn't a kid anymore."

Vince sobered and sat on the recliner facing a flat screen TV. "That's true. We know you never had sexual feelings toward her as a girl, but you can't deny you've always been taken with her. I remember when she played in Dallas the Christmas before you married Raquel. I had to practically hogtie you to keep you from making a jackass of yourself when those two security guards wouldn't let you backstage."

"I wanted to say howdy." He would never admit how enthralled he'd been by the eighteen-year-old woman as she belted out her hit-making country pop songs to a stadium full of screaming fans. She still ensnared him in her beauty. Frustrated at himself for letting his brothers' teasing bother him and for his foolish behavior, he headed toward the kitchen.

He could never admit he destroyed her speeding ticket. Hadn't he done it to be able to see her again? "That's all I was doing tonight. Being neighborly. I've had about enough of you two hayseeds. I'm collecting my son and going home."

Their snickers followed him into his sister-in-law's domain. EJ and Vince's wife, Clare, had gone to school together, and she and Raquel had been best friends. The petite blonde turned away from the stove after setting a large pan of lasagna on the burner. Before she had a chance to greet him with more than a bright smile, his other sister-in-law, Judy, grinned at him from the counter where she tossed a huge bowl of salad.

"Hope those meatheads haven't been tormenting you too much." Judy wiped her hands on her apron and stepped over to him. The curvy brunette hugged him. "You doin' okay?"

Judy and Tucker had finally gotten married three years ago after more than fifteen years of an on-again/off-again relationship. When she was younger, she had a reputation of being easy, which working at the local honky-tonk hadn't helped. Having three kids with Tucker before he'd actually put a ring on her finger hadn't improved her standing among the more snobbish folks in town either. Despite her own wild ways, she was good for his beer-drinking, rowdy brother, even if Tucker didn't always agree.

EJ knew she was asking about his mental state and returned her embrace. "I'm good."

Clare stood beside him with her hand on his arm, offering her own quiet support. "Glenda called me today."

He moved away from the women and narrowed his eyes on Clare. "What did she want?"

If his mother-in-law harassed Raquel's friends, he would have a nice long chat with her. Enough was enough. His wife was dead and this constant reminding everyone who had known her of the fact wasn't healthy.

Clare frowned and folded her arms over her rounded belly. She was about eight months pregnant with her and Vince's second child. Their son was the same age as Austin. "Glenda wanted me to convince you to go to dinner at the Marshalls' place."

EJ fisted his hands at his sides and gritted his teeth. "I already told Trevor I wasn't coming to dinner. Where's Austin? I'm going home."

Clare took a step toward him. "Why not stay here for dinner? You and Austin are always welcome."

He glanced from the women's hopeful expressions to the massive pan of lasagna. His brothers stood in the doorway between the big country kitchen and the living room. From the TV room their kids were laughing and making a general ruckus. Did he want to go home to an empty house and be alone?

He let out a breath as he met Clare's compassionate blue eyes, then nodded. "Okay." With a smile, he looked around the room again, taken aback by the relief radiating from his family. "Let's eat. I'm starved."

Vince and Tucker cuffed him on the shoulders as they passed him to the large trestle table set with an army of plates.

"Because sitting in that big office of yours is hard work," Tucker winked at him as he sat in the same place where he'd sat since they were kids.

"Daddy!" Austin ran into the kitchen with the other kids and bounded up into his lap.

"Hey, buddy." Hugging his son close, EJ kissed his forehead and ruffled his white-blond hair. He turned back to his smirking brother. As he considered his comeback to the familiar barb, the memory of stopping Emily in her fancy sports car and the confusion thinking about her had caused him all day flooded his mind. "Trust me I'd love to see you dealing with a speeder with a chip on his or her shoulder any day." *Not to mention the county's distrust.* Judy dragged over a highchair and set it beside him. As he sat Austin in the chair, he thanked her, then changed the subject. "I think we should eat. That lasagna smells delicious."

Chapter 6

The next morning, Emily sat at the kitchen table and ate eggs, bacon, and wholegrain toast her mother prepared.

Momma sipped her coffee. "I can't believe you never have any morning sickness. When I was pregnant with you, I was sick nearly the whole time. Her pregnancy with Johny was a little easier, but not by much."

Setting her fork on her empty plate, she shrugged. "I never thought about it. I'm glad I don't, though." She picked up her cup of English breakfast tea and stared into the dark brew. "Going through withdrawal was bad enough. I can't imagine what it would have been like to be puking all the time, too."

Her mother fiddled with the end of her braid lying over her shoulder. "I'm sorry. I shouldn't have brought it up."

Emily took a long sip of the honey-sweetened tea, then set down her mug. "Momma, you shouldn't have to filter your conversation with me. Besides, I don't want you to. I'm a recovering addict. I've made progress to getting back to my old self, but I can never forget where I was a few short months ago. I need to remember the pain of withdrawal and the clarity that came to me after it."

With a wide smile, Momma reached over the table and took Emily's hand into hers. "I love you. We'll get through this."

Emily rested her other hand over her mother's and squeezed. "I know we will." She pulled her hands away and took a deep breath. "I'd like to go into town. Is Johnson's Western still open?"

Her mother sniffed and nodded. "Yes. Would you like me to go with you?"

She shook her head and picked up her empty plate and mug. "I'm fine going by myself. I want to buy new boots and some Wranglers." She deposited her dishes in the sink and smiled over her shoulder at her mother's crinkled brow. "I don't even own a pair of boots without at least a six-inch heel. Nor do I have a pair of jeans that doesn't have some French designer name and cost more than most people around here make in a week." As she spoke, she lost the smile and heat rose on her face. She looked out the window, not able to face her mother's furrowed brow.

"Wow." Emily shook her head and turned to lean against the counter. "I'm out of touch with the world."

Her mother came to her and wrapped her up into a hug. "You were lost for a long time. But you're finding your way back."

Although Emily was at least three inches taller than her mom, Momma tucked her head into the crook of her neck, and she breathed in the comforting scent of lilies and vanilla. Fragrances she'd always associated with Momma. After a moment, Emily pulled away and changed the subject. "When's Dad leaving for his tour?"

Momma sniffed and poured a cup of coffee. "He's planning to leave the Monday after July fourth." She sipped from her mug. "Oh, I almost forgot. Tucker invited all of us to his brother's birthday party on the evening of the fourth. The Cowleys are having a barbecue at Tucker's place."

"Sure. Sounds fun." A tingling thrill flowed through her. She knew which Cowley brother had an Independence Day birthday--EJ. She busied herself with rinsing her breakfast dishes. "How long has EJ been sheriff?"

Her mother shrugged and sipped her coffee. "A little over two years. He was elected not long after getting out of the Army. Then his wife died from an overdose of depression medicine." She looked at Emily. "I saw you talking in the pasture last evening."

Emily stacked her dishes in the dishwasher. "He was saying hi. When I was younger we were friends."

Her mother smiled and set her mug on the counter. "I seem to remember you having one heck of a crush on him."

Heat scalded her cheeks. "Momma. I was--God, what was I?--like eleven years old."

"Yeah, well, I had a crush on your father since I was five years old and you see where that got me." Her mother's dark eyes twinkled with her amusement.

"Not going to happen." Emily laughed as she shut the dishwasher door. "EJ and I aren't you and Dad. He never considered me more than a pain-in-the-ass-kid who liked to follow him around. I was surprised he even stopped to say anything to me." What was going on with EJ? Why had he stopped, and more importantly, why did he get rid of the speeding ticket? She saw the interest in his gaze. God knew he intrigued her, but she couldn't let anything happen between them.

Before she had a chance to change the subject to something not as unsettling as EJ Cowley, a knock sounded on the kitchen door. Momma glanced at the clock on the six-burner range. "Oh darn, that must be Tucker and Vince. I have a meeting with them in less than five minutes."

Emily opened the door to the two men, who looked like older versions of their younger brother with a few variations. Tucker had dark hair, with dark brown eyes, while Vince looked like an identical older version of EJ, but with blue eyes instead of gray. They smiled and removed their hats as they entered the kitchen.

She gave each man a quick hug, causing them both to blush. "It's good to see you both."

Tucker was the first to recover from the unaccustomed greeting. "You too, Emily. How're you doing?"

She glanced at her mom. "A lot better now that I'm home."

A few moments later, she left her mother to her manager's duties. She found her old Stetson and sunglasses. It wasn't much of a disguise, but it would help her blend more with everyone else. Wishing she'd asked her mother if she could have borrowed her truck, she grabbed her car keys. Maybe she should think about trading the Maserati in for a more practical vehicle. The thought was fleeting as she headed to town with the top down and sang at the top of her lungs with the blasting country station on the radio--but she made sure she didn't venture more than five miles over the speed limits.

* * * *

Johnson's Western was exactly how Emily remembered it. The general store sold everything from exclusive western brand clothes, hats, and boots to the everyday basics like bread, milk, and eggs.

With more frustration than she'd ever experienced while shopping, she tried on two pairs of jeans. The first pair, in the size she'd worn for more than five years, didn't fit at all. The second, fit around her expanding belly, but were too baggy to be comfortable. She needed maternity pants, but how could she buy them without the news showing up in the next issue of some tabloid? The store had one or two other customers that she'd seen. She avoided the men by keeping her hat pulled over her face and staying away from the hunting aisle where they were looking at the guns with Mr. Johnson's help. Two teenage clerks stationed at the front checkout counters ignored her when she entered the store. As they restocked the candy self, the girls gossiped about someone cheating on her boyfriend.

She refolded the two pairs and headed out to the display of jeans. As she put the pants back into their slots, she glanced around to see if anyone was close enough to see her. Her heart pounded in time with the fast beat of the song playing over the sound system as she reached the cubbyholes marked maternity. With another discreet look around, she picked out three pairs in her size and headed back to the tiny dressing room.

The jeans fit perfectly, but how the hell was she going to buy them? She refolded the pants, tucked them under her arm, and went to the shoe section. While she looked for a pair of boots, she devised a plan. If she was lucky, maybe no one would notice she'd bought maternity jeans.

"I personally like Justin boots, but I work in mine."

She sucked in a breath at the low timbre of EJ's voice behind her. Was he everywhere in this town? Turning with a box of boots, she smiled. "It would seem that we have something in common then. I've always like them, too."

He raised a brow and a side of his mouth quirked up when he noticed the boots she'd chosen. A basic pair used mostly for riding and work. "You taking up cowboying now?"

She set the clothes she'd chosen on the bench beside her and sat to try on the boots. As she slipped off her flip-flops, she dug a pair of socks out of her purse. "Not that it's any of your business, but I need a pair of boots to ride in." She looked up at him with a smug smile. "Now that you know why I'm here." She looked over his uniform. Tan polyester blend shouldn't fit a man that sinfully well. "You're obviously working. I want to know why you're following me."

He rubbed a hand over his chin and averted his gaze. "I...eh... Saw you come into the store and wanted to ask if you'd join me for coffee."

Was he asking her out on a date? Trying hard and failing to stop her heart from speeding up at the possibility, she pulled on her socks. "I don't drink coffee."

"Well, then I guess you'll have to join me for lunch."

As she tugged on one of the boots, she looked up at him. His pewter eyes held a challenge in them. She pulled on the other one and stood. Damn, they were too tight. Ignoring the pinching of the boots, she put her hands on her hips. "Tell you what. You can drink coffee and I'll drink tea, how does that sound? I had breakfast not too long ago."

He glanced at her feet, then knelt down in front of her.

"What are you doing?" She took a step back, but he caught her foot.

"You look like you're trying to stuff your feet into a shoe three sizes too small." He squeezed around her booted foot, then glanced up at her. "Boots are supposed to fit like a glove not a vise."

Holy hell, he looked hot down there. She couldn't get enough air in her lungs.

EJ stood and pulled the next size off the self. "Try these."

He was close enough that every breath she took filled her senses with his clean outdoorsy scent. How could a man smell this good?

"Are you a boot salesman as well as the sheriff?" Did that husky voice belong to her?

"I know something about boots." He grinned, showing off straight white teeth and full kissable lips.

Stepping back, she bumped into her pile of clothes on the bench, knocking them to the floor in front of him. Before she could bend to pick them up, he knelt and gathered up a pair of the jeans. When he shifted his surprised gaze to hers, she trembled as icy fear replaced the heat of attraction in her gut.

She knelt next to him and took a deep breath. In a low tone, she said, "Yes, I'm pregnant, but I'm not ready to let it be common knowledge."

He refolded the jeans and set them on the bench. "Then your secret is safe with me. How were you planning to buy these? The clerk would see what they are."

She set a folded pair on top of the one he'd placed on the bench and shifted to sit beside them. "I know. I was hoping I could distract her enough that she wouldn't notice what she was ringing through."

He leaned against the shelf of boots behind him. "Not a half-bad plan."

Needing to do something besides stare at him, she lifted one of the boots out of the box he'd given her and pulled it on. A much better fit. She slipped into the other boot.

"You could let me buy them."

She swung her gaze to him. "What?"

He shrugged and pushed away from the wall. The overhead light glinted on the star pinned to his uniform shirt. "I'll tell the girl at the register that they're for the church mission. They've been collecting things for weeks now for the poor, and this wouldn't be the first time I bought stuff for it."

Her heart jumped at the idea of EJ being such generous person.

He reached for the jeans, but she rested her hand over his. The contact sent a warm liquid sensation through her palm. "Why are you doing this?"

"Because I don't give a damn if people gossip about me. I'm used to it." He pulled the stack of pants out from under her hand. "Besides, if their talking about me buying women's pants for the mission, they aren't criticizing me for how I'm doing my job."

She stood and folded her arms under her breasts. "Why would they do that?"

He shook his head and smiled, but his beautiful eyes darkened. "That's a story for another time." Jutting his chin toward the boots on her feet, he asked, "How do they fit?"

"Like a glove." She smiled and touched his arm. As the muscle beneath her fingers bunched and released, a sliver of delight tingled through her at the touch. He glanced at her hand, and when he looked up at her, the cold pewter of his eyes took on a molten glow. She dropped her hand and swallowed hard. "I'll meet you over at the diner. At least I owe you lunch."

"Thought you weren't hungry."

She shrugged and bent to pull off one of the boots. "I am now."

* * * *

What the hell was he doing?

EJ sat in his Tahoe while Emily parked behind him on the street in front of the Chow House Restaurant on Amarillo Street. He wasn't sure what possessed him to follow Emily into Johnson's Western, let alone buy her pants. Glancing at the green plastic bag beside him on the seat, he took a deep breath and blew it out between clenched teeth. He was a damned fool. Besides being way out of his league and a recovering drug addict, she was pregnant with another man's baby.

Did he honestly want to be messed up with her? He should tell her he got a call and get the hell away from her. Through her reflection in his rearview mirror, he watched Emily get out of her car to wait for him. Still trying to come up with an excuse to escape, he picked up the sack holding her clothes and opened his door.

With a look around to make sure no one saw, he handed her the shopping bag. She took it and smiled. "Thank you again, EJ. You didn't have to do this."

He wasn't going anywhere. God help him, but he did want to get to know her again and be her friend if nothing else. "It was nothing. Friends help friends."

Her intense jade eyes widened. "Is that what we are?"

"I'd like to be your friend, Emily." He put his hands into his pockets to squelch the sudden desire to touch her. "I have a feeling you don't have many."

With an unwavering gaze, she studied him for a moment. "I'd like to be yours, too." She fished out the receipt from the bag before tossing the package onto her side seat. After getting her wallet out, she pulled out a hundred dollar bill and some change, then held it out to him. "I have a feeling you don't have many either."

He took the repayment for her clothes and snickered as he looked at the money in his hand. "This has to be the weirdest thing I've ever done."

"Me too." She tilted her head toward the front door of the diner. "C'mon. I'm suddenly famished."

Inside the restaurant, they found a corner table. EJ slid into the booth, but before Emily had the chance to sit, several employees and costumers surrounded her. As she had done at the checkout at the general store, she posed for pictures, and signed autographs as the fans wished her happiness and a quick recovery. How many of the gushing girls and women noticed her bright smile never reached her eyes?

A few moments later, the people dispersed, going back to work or to their half-eaten meals.

"My name's Rory." A young waitress, who was the daughter of the owners, laid two menus on the table. She stepped back and fidgeted with her pad and pen. "I love you. Wow. I can't believe you're here in my restaurant. Will you sign my pad? Please."

"Sure. Rory, right?" The girl nodded and smiled widely. Emily took the girl's pad and signed it. "This is my hometown."

Rory giggled as she took the tablet back and held it to her chest. "I know. How awesome is that?"

With a smile that seemed bright and dead at the same time, Emily moved into the booth.

"*Follow your dreams. Love, Emily Kendall,*" read the girl in an awestruck voice she might have used to speak to God Himself. She stared at Emily's sprawled message for a moment. "Wow. Thank you!"

"You're welcome." With a smile, Emily opened the menu. "I think I'm ready to order. EJ?"

"Okay." Rory flipped the pages to a blank and dropped her pen. "Oops. Sorry about that."

"I'm good. Go ahead when Rory's all set." He had no idea what he wanted to eat. The experience with Emily had him rattled almost as badly as it did poor Rory. But for him, he had a sudden desire to protect her from all the prying eyes and the nervous waitress. No wonder she seemed relieved when he'd offered to buy her jeans on a whim. Seeing the fear in her eyes when he'd noticed the maternity sizes had caused a weight to settle in his gut. Was this what her life was like?

She closed her menu. "I'd like the American burger with a side of French fries and sweet tea."

Surprised by her order, he raised a brow and smiled. "I'll have the same thing."

Rory grinned and looked from him to Emily as she took their menus. "Are y'all friends?"

Emily nodded. "Yes. We've known each other since we were kids."

"Wow." Rory shook her head as if trying to get her starstruck brain to function. "I'll be right back with your teas."

"Sorry about all that," Emily said when the girl was out of earshot. She fussed with the silverware on the paper placemat advertising various local businesses. "I should have known what coming in here would be like."

Before he had a chance to answer, Rory brought two tall glasses of iced tea and set them on the table. Thankfully, she scurried away before she had a chance to gush over Emily any more than she already had.

He propped his elbows on the table and rested his chin on his folded hands. "Does this kind of thing happen to you everywhere you go? Because if it does, what a royal pain in the behind."

She laughed, and the sound, all husky and sexy, landed somewhere low in his belly. "I can't go anywhere without being noticed. I've gotten good at disguises. I even have a few wigs I've worn when I don't want anyone to recognize me. But then I run the chance of being noticed and people thinking I've changed my hair, or worse."

He leaned back in his seat. "How the hell do you stand it?"

With a shrug, she looked around the room at the people still staring at her. When she turned her gaze to his, her eyes held a shadow. "To be perfectly honest, I have no idea how I'll deal with it. For the past couple years, I've always been too... eh... high to care."

Her honesty had him blinking. "How did you handle it before? You've been famous for a long time."

"Thanks for being diplomatic." She picked up her tea and gave him a mock toast, then took a sip.

Did she wish it was something stronger?

Sighing, she set the glass down and played with the condensation on the surface. "When I first started getting popular, I had my dad. I think he protected me a lot from the price of being a celebrity. Then I started touring on my own and rebelling against what I considered his control over me, I..." She took a deep breath and shrugged.

"That's about the same time you met the rock star." Who, if the tabloids could be trusted, had introduced her to the drugs.

She nodded. "I never handled my fame well. I love my fans, but now I miss being..."

As her quiet voice trailed away, something in her tone had him reaching for her hand. She snapped her gaze to his, and he squeezed her cold fingers. "You want to be normal."

"More than anyone can guess. Singing was--is--my dream, but sometimes I wish I'd listened to my dad and waited until I was older. Being famous at such a young age wasn't easy."

He swallowed and leaned forward. "You know in a weird way, we have something in common. I wasn't a teenager, but I remember my first firefight, and I wasn't ready for it. I had graduated college and deployed to the Middle East. ISIS was making a mess of things, and I was part of an intelligence mission sent to find out their next target." As the memories of his first battle flooded him, he shook his head and closed his eyes to make the images stop. Despite his best intentions, he relived the moment he fired his M16 and watched the bullet as it hit the first man he'd ever shot. For years, he heard the cries of the two wounded soldiers in his unit before they died. What had possessed him to bring up his Army days? Fearing for his life and killing other humans was nothing like her life of fame and wealth.

At her gentle touch on his hand, he opened his eyes and met her haunted gaze. "I remember hearing about that fight. I was afraid for you."

Her quiet voice vibrated through him. At most, she'd been fifteen years old back then. "But that was about the same time your first record came out."

She smiled and nodded as her eyes took on a heavy-lidded look which couldn't be anything except desire. "You were my friend and I worried about you."

He'd never wanted anything as much as he wanted to kiss her right now.

Rory brought their burgers, breaking the sudden trance pulling him under.

Emily let go of his hand and straightened in her seat. "These look delicious. Thank you, Rory."

While EJ sat for a moment in a daze, Emily picked up a French fry and popped it in her mouth as she watched him. He had to get away from her before he did something extremely stupid.

She sipped her tea. "What time do you get off duty?"

"Four." His voice sounded rough even to his ears. "Why?"

"Would you like to join me for a ride through the pasture?"

His heart sped up at the invitation. "Sounds fun."

She smiled, and this time, it lit up her eyes. "Good."

So much for staying the hell away from her.

Chapter 7

When they reached the riverbank, Emily pulled up and turned in her saddle as EJ came up beside her. Looking sexier than any man had the right to in a plaid western shirt and faded jeans, he leaned over his saddle. He patted the neck of the big gray gelding he'd borrowed from his brother Vince.

"I haven't been out here in years." EJ swung out of the saddle, his feet hitting the dirt with a thud.

"Me either." She moved to dismount her horse.

"Wait. I'll help you out of the saddle." He came up beside Tinkerbell and put his hands on her waist.

"I can get off a horse by myself." The heat of his touch warmed her up faster than the ninety degree temperature of the afternoon had.

His eyes darkened under the brim of his hat as he looked up at her. "I don't want you to fall."

Before she could protest, he lifted her out of the saddle. She slid down the length of his hard body and gasped when her feet finally hit the ground at the erotic sensations tingling over her. They stood touching from chest to thighs and staring into each other's eyes for what seemed like forever before he let her go. As he took a deep breath, he turned away, but she noticed the telltale bulge in his jeans.

Dear God, he was as turned on as she was.

She gulped in air and shook herself, then moved away from the horses to watch the orange light of the late afternoon sun skip over the slow flowing water of the Salt Fork of the Red River. A soft warm breeze rustled through the live oaks and a cow lowed somewhere in the pasture. Not having an idea how to shatter the sudden charged tension between them, she wrapped her arms around herself and closed her eyes.

"I remember when you used come here when you were a kid." His husky voice had her facing him. As he sat on a boulder sitting by a trunk of a large oak, he jutted his thumb toward a stand of trees about a hundred yards down the riverbank. "I had a treehouse in that big ponderosa over there. Did you know when you first started sneaking over to the Double K, I would sit up there and watch you?"

She sat on the soft moss growing over the exposed roots of the tree next to his rock. After she drew her legs up and hugged them to her chest, she rested her cheek on her knees and smiled at him. "No, I didn't know. But I must admit, considering our age difference, that bit of information is--well--creepy."

He chuckled and took his hat off to hold between his hands. "True. Although my interest was chivalrous, I think. I was afraid you'd fall into the water and get hurt. You were such a damn daredevil."

The sweetness of his confession sent a tingling thrill dance over her nerves. "You shouldn't have worried too much. I mostly came over here to watch the river and think up songs."

She looked out over the sluggish river. The water appeared muddy, but the appearance was an illusion created from the reddish yellow slit lining the bottom. A memory brought a bittersweet knot to her throat. "The first song Dad and I ever wrote together was under this tree." She turned to him. "He used to come here to write songs, too. I found him here one morning, and we ended up writing *The Long Road Home* together." They'd sung the song at the county fair later that fall, but before they'd gone on stage, he'd announced she was his daughter to over ten thousand people. The song later became her first number one and began her career. She took a deep breath and looked back at him. "I didn't know he was my dad when we wrote it."

He touched her shoulder. "I can't imagine finding out you've been lied to. Me and my whole family were shocked when we heard the news."

She took his hand and held it. He stiffened, and she thought he wanted to pull away, but he soon relaxed and squeezed her fingers. "I didn't know who I was for a long time. Then when Mike went on trial and all of his secrets came out, I had to accept I was a pawn in his sick games. I agreed to take Seth's name legally, not just professionally."

Seth had wanted to legally adopt her, but she hadn't been sure until Mike's trial.

The sting in her eyes came fast and furious. "Mike hated me. He admitted he wished he'd either killed me or had me kidnapped when I was little."

* * * *

EJ swallowed hard, but the lump in his throat wouldn't budge. For as long as he'd been sheriff, he'd held a deep dislike for the man who'd caused him distrust by the people he'd sworn to protect. But now he hated the man. No wonder the beautiful, carefree girl he remembered turned into such a mess as an adult. "Mike was a sick man, Emily. I know it doesn't make what he did easier, but you don't have to let it define you. You're too strong for that."

She blinked causing moisture to gather on her eyelashes like dew clinging to blades of grass. But she didn't shed any tears. "I hope you're right." She laid her hand over her belly. How did she hide her pregnancy? Her abdomen definitely had a telling curve. "I need to be strong for my baby. Life won't be easy for either of us."

What role would the father play in the child's life? Who was the father--her ex or someone else? He pulled the reins on his curiosity before he asked. She didn't owe him an explanation, and he was deep enough in this quicksand bog already.

After a moment, she said, "Back at the store you said you're used to people gossiping about you. What did that mean?"

As she regarded him with eyes as green as the moss on the tree, the evening sun turned her short auburn hair a burnished copper color. He fought the impulse to run his fingers through it. Instead, he filled his lungs with earthy scented air and put his hat on his head. "Mike Ritter ruined the office of sheriff for this county. No one trusts me. I think at first they may have because I'm a vet. But then Raquel committed suicide and a lot of people blame me for it. They think I've covered up what actually happened."

She narrowed her eyes. "They're fools. I didn't know Raquel well, but I know you. You'd never do anything to hurt her."

Her determined tone spread warmth though him. If she only knew how he'd covered up where Raquel had gotten the depression pills, she wouldn't be sure of herself. He stood and held out his hand. "C'mon, we had better be getting back. It's a long ride and the sun is setting fast."

She put her hand into his. The sensation of her smooth skin in his grasp stirred his desire again. "You're right. Let's go."

Chapter 8

On Saturday afternoon, Gabe McKenna arrived with Emily's things. Her father's best friend unloaded a crate holding her ten CMA awards. Of all her various accolades, the CMA crystal statue she won for Best New Artist six months after her debut album went double platinum was the one she valued the most, because it was her first award. Her father followed him with the last crate, which held her six Grammy figurines. Four other crates held her other twenty-three awards and the plaques for her gold and platinum records.

They set their crates with the other ones on the floor of the den outside her father's recording studio. Emily handed them each a glass of lemonade. Gabe sat in a leather captain's chair, while she and her dad sat on the couch across from him. Gabe looked around at the wooden crates and snickered. "I've been in this business a lot longer than you and don't have this many awards. I'm jealous."

Her dad laughed. "Me, too. Where the heck are we going to put them all?" With a shake of his head, he glanced at her. "I'll have to build onto the house to have room to display them all."

Despite his words, the shimmer of raw pride in his gaze humbled her, and a blush burned her cheeks. "I don't expect to display them. I haven't for years, but didn't want to send them to storage in Nashville either."

Dad sipped his lemonade, then jutted his chin toward one of the lighted glass cases where some of his various honors were displayed. "I think you should put out your favorites. Those that mean the most to you. We can make room for them easily enough in the cabinets with mine."

"That would be great." She cleared her throat and set her glass on the coffee table. "Gabe, Dad told me why you were willing to drive out of your way to bring my stuff. Thank you for doing this for me."

"You're welcome. I told you I'd do anything for you and would have done it even if I hadn't wanted to talk to your dad." He glanced at her father. "He told you he's being stubborn about joining me."

"Yes. Now, I want to hear what you have planned." She clasped her hands in front of her.

"Emily?"

At her father's questioning tone, she looked from Gabe to her father. "I think what you told me is a fantastic idea. I want to learn more."

Gabe shifted in his seat and leaned over his legs. "It's simple. I want Seth to go into business with me to form our own label." He looked around the room and at the studio behind a wall of soundproof windows. "Hell, we could record right here until we can rent studio time or set up our own in Nashville. Might actually be cheaper to fly an artist here to record than rent space in the city." He grinned at her dad. "Your setup is better than some of the studios in Nashville."

"That's crazy." Her father shook his head. "No one would come here to record. How about session musicians? What makes it possible for me to record here is that the music is produced for the most part in Nashville."

"What about the local guys? You've been using them for years," Emily said, referring to a local band called Lawman. None of the men wanted the headache of fame, which her father had offered them--more than once over the years. The band made up of mostly local law enforcement was good enough to make it in Nashville. They played and sang on most of her father's records and no one knew they weren't professional session musicians.

Emily didn't understand why her dad was against the idea or his attachment to Midland Records. "And even if Lawman didn't want the job, I bet we could find professional quality musicians right around here."

"We?" Gabe raised a brow. "What are you hinting at?"

She took a deep breath and let it out. "I've been thinking about this idea since Dad told me about it, and I want in on the deal. Dad mentioned his concern about financing and startup costs. Well, I think I can definitely help with that. I've never spent a dime of the considerable trust funds both my grandfather and Dad set up for me. I think investing it into a promising company is the best thing I can do with the money."

"Wow." Gabe sat back in his chair. "I didn't see this coming. But aren't you in the middle of recording your next album?"

She rubbed her palms on her thighs. "I've asked Trish this morning to negotiate with Paul to get me out of my contract. Midland can release what I've done as an EP."

Gabe whistled. "You're giving up the whole pop scene?"

Her father looked as surprised by her announcement as Gabe did. "Are you thinking of switching back to country?"

She smiled and shrugged. "I'm thinking of retiring from performing, but I don't want to give up music. I could never do that. It's too much a part of me. This scheme seems to be the perfect answer."

Dad rubbed his jaw like he did when considering something. "I *am* worried about the startup cost, but I'm also wondering where we're going to get artists. My album released a month ago, and I know you finished up one," he said and nodded toward Gabe. "Besides, I'm not sure breaking our contracts with Midland won't end up costing us money in legal fees."

Gabe finished his lemonade and set the tumbler on the glass-topped coffee table. "I agree getting away from Midland isn't going to be easy. But I'm not concerned Paul won't let us go. As for artists, I have two in mind. The first I met at the Bluebird Café. Jared Wafford is a college kid who comes to Nashville on the weekends to play the bars hoping to catch the eye of a record producer. I asked him for a demo and can play it for you." He sat back in his seat. "The second singer is Cara Alexander."

"I know her," Emily said. "She co-wrote with me for my first pop record. Amazing talent--both as a songwriter and singer--but she's struggled with hitting the charts and keeping a record company."

"If she's a diva, I don't think we should even consider her," Dad said.

With a shake of his head, Gabe leaned forward again. "Cara's having trouble because she had a manager who steered her the wrong way. She's from a small farm in Alabama and is as country as you or me. When I saw her at The Listening Room, she sang covers from some of the most famous ladies in the genre." He grinned at Emily. "She even sang one of your early hits."

She laughed and folded her legs under her. "Let me guess. *Leave Me a Rose.* Cara loves that song. I know she wants to break into country. I say we consider her. She has some established fan base that might follow her over, especially if we help her find songs bridging the genres. Kinda what my last country album did, except in reverse."

When she finished talking, both men stared at her. She shifted in her seat and looked from one to the other. "What?"

Her dad laughed and patted her knee. "I think we found our producer."

"*Me?*" she squeaked and a thrill tingled over her skin.

Dad wrapped his arm around her shoulders, pulling her into a hug. "I think all we need now is a name for the label."

"That will come. Let's celebrate first." Gabe stretched his long legs and stood. "What's the name of that local watering hole?" He lost the grin and a blush colored his expression. "Oh, damn. I'm sorry, Emily. I didn't mean…"

"I think Gatlin's is perfect," she said.

Gabe shook his head. "No, we can go out to dinner somewhere."

She saved him from embarrassment. Being around booze was hard, but she had a good reason to stay sober, and she didn't plan on ever going back. She stood and smiled. "I guess I should let you in on the secret since we are business partners. Even if I hadn't turned my life around this time in rehab, I have no intention of drinking or doing anything else." She rested both hands over her belly. "What I'm about to tell you isn't public, and I want to keep it that way for as long as physically possible."

Gabe furrowed his brows, then widened his eyes. "Holy shit, you're pregnant."

* * * *

EJ and three other deputies parked their Tahoes as close as they could get and trudged the quarter mile to the local honky-tonk. People stood in the parking lot, screaming and making general fools of themselves. Lawman was a great band, but they never generated this much of a ruckus. Heck, even Seth Kendall no longer caused more than an excited clatter when he occasionally played Gatlin's.

Deputy Billy Collins whistled as he came to a stop beside EJ. "Who is playing here?"

Only one person he knew of could cause this much trouble. The other day in town, he'd stood back while people swarmed Emily Kendall. He'd also attended a few of her concerts. They were wild and massive events. Surely, she wouldn't be here. His heart sped up at the thought of seeing her again. Irritated at his reaction as much as this out-of-control crowd, he turned to the deputies. "Get these people out of here. I'll go inside and clear some of them out of the bar. Then I'm going home."

As his deputies acknowledged the order and fanned out, he pushed his way through a group of young women, who didn't look old enough to step foot into the bar, and found the bouncer, Earl Murphy, guarding the door. The older man had been as much a mainstay at the joint as old man Gatlin himself.

"Hey, Earl, what the hell is going on?" From the sounds of loud music and the cheering crowd inside, a major concert was happening.

Earl had to be pushing sixty years old, but he was still as big as a grizzly bear and looked as mad as one, too. He narrowed his gaze on an obvious teenage girl trying to sneak around him to get inside. She backed away, and he glared at EJ as he bit out, "Seth and Emily Kendall and freaking Gabe McKenna showed up at the same time and decided they'd all sing. The moment every teenybopper within twenty miles heard Emily Kendall and Gabe McKenna were here all hell broke loose."

EJ pinched his brows together. Why would a recovering alcoholic risk the temptation by going to a bar? "The bartender called us." The deputies worked to wrangle the disgruntled mass back to their cars. Two more teenagers tried to sneak past him, and Earl stopped them with a dark scowl. Would cats would be this wily? He supposed he was about to find out and tipped his hat toward the door. "Can I get in?"

Earl turned a worried glance at the entrance. "What's one more person? The place is already a fire hazard."

Gatlin's was one of the largest honky-tonks outside of Amarillo and a popular place for top-notch entertainment. If one of the local bands wasn't playing, Jimmy Gatlin booked the latest country acts through sponsorships with two local radio stations and with help from Seth Kendall.

He shoved his way through the sea of bodies. The scents of sweat, perfume, and beer pressed in on him as much as the gyrating crowd. Ignoring the stage as the men sang a rowdy song they'd released a few years ago, EJ shoved and threatened several people crowding around at the door to leave the bar. After he cleared the area, he shifted his attention to another group standing in the space between the large oak horseshoe shaped bar and the tables. The men finished their song to shouts and wild applause from the audience. EJ forced several more bystanders to leave, until only a few people stood along the perimeters. Figuring his job complete, he headed for the door.

"How y'all doin' tonight?"

The familiar smoky voice stopped him cold. EJ turned to find Emily at the microphone. The remaining audience cheered, and the sexiest woman he'd ever known smiled at him. She was a vision dressed in a short, high-wasted summer dress and a pair of sky-high strappy sandals that made her long legs seem to go on forever.

"I see Sheriff Cowley cleared a few folks out to give us all some extra breathing room." She shifted the strap of the glittery lavender guitar she'd made famous onto her shoulder. "We love that y'all are as excited about us being here as we are, but Gatlin's isn't AT & T Stadium." The crowd whistled and another cheer shook the walls. "Let's give Sheriff Cowley and his deputies a round of applause for keeping us safe."

She held up her hands and clapped, encouraging the rest of the people to do the same. A few older folks patted him on the shoulder and shook his hand, Jimmy Gatlin being one of them. His bother Tucker waved him over to a table near the packed dance floor. Vince produced an extra chair from somewhere and Tucker ordered him a beer. EJ sat between his brothers' wives, quickly greeting the women, then looked back up at the stage as Emily spoke again to the audience.

"This first song has never been recorded. I wrote *A Soldier's Glory* about six years ago when a friend of mine was sent to the Middle East for the first time." When Emily winked at him, his heart stuttered over a beat.

She turned to her dad, who was acting as her lead guitarist, and the rest of the band, made up of Lawman and Gabe McKenna. After talking a few moments to the musicians and playing a few chords on her guitar as if she was instructing them, she led them in an opening of a song that couldn't be anything but country. EJ tried to puzzle through her meaning--had he been the friend? The timing was too right for his deployment to be a coincidence. Rowdy applause jerked him back into the present.

She closed her eyes and leaned into the mic as she sang the beginning of the ballad,

"I was a girl with a beat-up guitar always tempting fate,
You were a boy in scuffed boots and a Stetson hat,
I chased my dreams of fortune and fame,
But you went away to find a soldier's glory."

He stared at Emily. There was no doubt who the song was about, and by the astonished stares turned in his direction, a lot of the locals figured it out as well.

"Damn, that song's about you and her," Vince said with a shake of his head.

"Shut it," EJ snapped as he picked up the beer the waitress had set in front of him and drained half of it. He ignored his brothers' smirks and listened to Emily sing of the pride she felt and of having faith in his safe return as he chased a soldier's glory.

She belted out the last notes of the patriotic tune, then the audience rose to its feet in a rousing ovation. EJ stood on rubbery legs and clapped. His heart ached at the sentiment in the song, the fact she wrote it for him, and chose tonight to sing it. He needed to talk to her.

She bowed, then with a wide smile, gestured a hand toward him.

As he sat down, he couldn't help the thoughts racing through his muddled mind.

What was she doing to him?

Chapter 9

Emily sang three more old songs. She loved every moment of it, but she wanted to talk to EJ. As he watched her, she couldn't stop looking at him, and by the time she finished the love song she recorded for her second album, there was no denying the intensity in his gray-eyed gaze or the way it heated her in places she didn't want it to.

With a wave, she thanked the audience and headed off the stage. As she put her guitar in its case, she watched EJ amble toward her. Her mouth dried up at the prospect of spending time with him.

He stopped a few feet away from her and fiddled with his hat between his hands. "You wrote a song about me?"

She folded her arms in front her and shrugged, going for nonchalance, but inside her belly flopped and her heart pounded at the prospect that he liked the song. "I wrote a lot of songs about a lot of people. Most notable are those I wrote about my two famous ex-boyfriends."

Before she married Fabian, she'd dated two teenage actors. Neither relationship had been serious, but the crap those two pretty boys put her through made good fodder for angsty breakup songs and even two or three revenge songs.

At his grin, her belly clinched at the way it transformed his handsome face to gorgeous. "I guess I should be glad my song wasn't like those." After a moment, he put his hat on his head. "I'll see you around."

When he turned to leave, her heart sank. She didn't want him to go. "EJ?"

He glanced over his shoulder at her, and a thrill surged through her at the invitation in his gaze. "You wanna get out of here?"

"Yeah. Let me tell my dad."

Getting to the door became almost impossible as the people stopped her, wanting autographs, cell phone pictures, or to give her their well wishes. She sensed EJ's growing discomfort at having the crowd of people press in on them. They were about halfway through the bar when he took her hand.

His warm, rough touch elicited a tingle of warmth to travel up her arm. She glanced at him. Why did he take her hand? Did he feel the same buzz she did?

As soon as they passed through the door, he let go of her. "I thought I'd never get out of there."

She took a deep breath and studied his profile as he stared out at the vehicles in the parking lot. Under the bright spotlights outside the bar, beads of sweat pooled on his forehead and his skin appeared pale beneath an enticing shadow of dark stubble. "Hey, are you okay?"

He swallowed hard enough to make his throat move and met her gaze. "I needed to get out of there or things would have been more than a little dicey."

What did that mean?

Before she had a chance to voice her question, he asked, "Is your car here?"

She tilted her head toward her father's crew cab Ram truck sitting at the side of the bar. "I came with Dad and Gabe. You'll have to drive."

The color was coming back into his cheeks, and he flashed his gorgeous, cocky-as-hell grin. "I came in my official rig."

She shrugged in an effort to hide the shiver coursing through her at the sudden desire heating her insides. "As long as the handcuffs are fuzzy, I'm game."

He chuckled as he took her hand again. "Fuzzy handcuffs, eh? I'll have to see what I can do about that."

As soon as EJ helped her into the passenger side, memories flashed through her mind of a time when she called a different man "Daddy" and she had no idea he was a monster.

They traveled toward McAllister in silence for a while. At the light in the center of town, EJ glanced at her. "You're awful quiet all of a sudden."

She sighed and rubbed her hands over the gooseflesh on her arms. "I was remembering all the times Mike drove me around in his sheriff's cruiser."

As the light changed to green, he nodded and turned onto River Street which eventually became River Road--the county cowpath they both lived along. "Did you ever hear from him after his trial?"

"Once. After he was sent to Clements Prison, I received a letter from him. Mom never let me read it." She looked down at her hands and fisted them on her thighs, fighting the pain the memories caused. "But I know what it said."

"I shouldn't have brought it up. I'm sorry." He glanced at her. "But if you ever want to talk about what your family did to you, I'm here to listen."

At the sudden burn in her sinuses, she wiped her nose with the back of her hand, refusing to let the bitterness bubble up. Could she talk to EJ about Mike and her parents? He met her gaze for a moment, and she saw something she'd not seen in the eyes of anyone who'd known her all of her life--compassion. Not pity, not guilt or hatred, but empathy. She'd learned through the last two years of forced counseling that not talking about her screwed-up feelings for the man she thought of as her father for all of her early childhood, and for the lie her mother told, or Seth's not fighting for her when she was little was much worse than keeping them locked up. Oh, she understood the messy reasons for all of it, but knowing why the events had happened wasn't the same as truly accepting them.

Before he had to look back at the street, she asked, "Am I crazy that a part of me still loves Mike, and another part hates my mom and dad?"

"You thought he was your father during some of your most influential years. As for your feelings for your mom and dad, I think that's understandable. Your mom lied to you. Your dad stayed away while he got rich and famous."

She snorted. "You make it sound simple."

"Isn't it?"

With a shrug, she looked out the side window as the houses of the town gave way to dark pastures. "I don't know. Some of the things I feel aren't that cut and dry. I do hate Mike more than I love him, and I love my parents more than I could ever despise them for their stupid mistakes they made when they were teenagers."

"You're more forgiving than I might be in your boots."

"I don't believe you." She looked back at him and met his gaze. With a smile, she laid her hand on his upper arm. The bicep under his shirt contracted at her touch, and their eyes met again. "I'm glad we're friends, EJ. I need one now."

Oh, they could easily be more than friends, if the heat in his gaze was any indication, but she couldn't let there be more than friendship between them. The feeling of loss hit her hard in the chest. God, she wished she could have *more*.

He smiled and looked back to the dark straight stretch of road, but soon a frown tugged his lips. "What were you doing at Gatlin's tonight?"

She bit her lip to keep the grin from her lips and folded her hands together in her lap. "Giving the sheriff's department a reason to practice mob control."

He snorted and flipped on the turn signal. "Funny." He pulled into his driveway and parked the SUV in front of a detached garage. The seriousness in his expression when he faced her took her aback. "Why would you risk the temptation?"

She sighed but couldn't be angry at his unspoken question: *Or haven't you given up the booze and drugs?* "The strongest thing I had to drink tonight was water. We were celebrating and decided the best way was by putting on a show."

EJ folded his arms over the top of the steering wheel and leaned in as he studied her. "Celebrating?"

She opened her door and gestured toward the outside with a tilt of her head. "C'mon. Let's get out of here and we can talk."

They left the SUV and headed up the stone walkway to the front porch of the two-story ranch house. He unlocked the door and turned on the light inside before shifting to the side for her to enter. After he hung his hat on a rack by the door, he motioned for her to follow him into the living room. "Sorry about the mess. I try to keep Austin's toys cleaned up, but I had to rush out this morning."

Chunky plastic construction trucks littered the floor between the couch and a built-in unit of shelves stacked with colorful crates filled with more toys. "Kids need to play. He's two, correct?" He nodded, and she added, "Where is he tonight?"

"With the Marshalls. I promised Glenda I'd let him visit for the weekend."

She couldn't help but wrinkle her nose. "I never liked that woman."

EJ laughed as he turned on a lamp next to the couch. "Not many people do. Try having her as a mother-in-law."

"No, thank you. You deserve a medal. When I was a teenager, I was friends with Trevor. She made such a stink about it he eventually told me we couldn't be friends anymore."

"Sounds like Glenda. If she can't control you, she finds ways to control those around you. The key to living with her is to make her think she has control." He jutted his chin toward the leather couch. "Have a seat. Would you like something to drink? I'm going to make a cup of coffee, but I can make you some tea."

Surprised by him remembering she didn't drink coffee, she raised a brow and sat on the edge of the couch. "I'd love tea. Thank you."

"Coming right up."

She watched him enter the kitchen at the back of the house. Her heart thumped in her chest at how easy and hard having a friendship with this man would be. She couldn't deny her attraction to him, but she could never let anything develop from it. Maybe she should leave. The Double K wasn't too far away, and she could always call her mom to come and get her. Momma hadn't come with them to Gatlin's, but elected to stay home with Johnny.

Emily reached into her purse to fish out her phone when EJ returned carrying a tray holding two steaming mugs, a bowl of sugar, and small milk pitcher. The only thing missing was a plate of cookies. The sight of such domesticity in a man who exuded hundred-proof testosterone struck her as hilarious, and she laughed.

He set the tray on the end table next to her. "What's funny?"

"I'm sorry…" She sucked in a breath, but couldn't control the giggles. "It's…"

As if he'd read the situation, he chuckled as he poured milk into the mug holding coffee, then picked it up. "Okay, a man with a tray is amusing, but my mama raised me in the height of good ol' Southern hospitality."

She wiped the corners of her eyes with the back of her hands and shook herself in an increased effort to get under control. When she finally did, she smiled at him. "I always liked your momma." She lifted the tea bag out of the cup of hot water a few times to help it brew. "She made the best banana nut muffins."

His mother had worked as her grandfather's housekeeper for years, while his dad was the Double K's foreman.

He sat in the chair next to the end table. "She loved to bake, but now she doesn't do much. Her arthritis is too bad."

"I'm sorry to hear it." She fixed her tea with sugar and laid the spoon on the tray.

"What were y'all celebrating tonight?"

Hugging the hot mug between her hands, she leaned back in her seat and sipped the sweet, soothing brew. "Gabe, Dad, and I are opening our own record label."

He whistled between his teeth. "Sounds impressive."

She shrugged setting the cup on the tray and outlined their plan.

"You're retiring from singing?"

Not being able to sit any longer, she stood and moved around the room to the entertainment unit sitting on the shelves of the built-in. She mindlessly brushed her fingers over his impressive collection of CDs, pulling an occasional case out to look at the cover art. "Maybe. I love performing, but I can't do it on a large scale anymore." The name on several of the cases gave her pause. She turned to look at him. "You have every one of my CDs?"

He stood and set his cup on the tray. "Yeah." He crossed the room to stop inches from her. This close, his masculine scent of sage and spice enveloped her, as did the heat in his pewter eyes. He brushed the back of his fingers over her cheek, and the sensation hit her as hard as a snort of pure coke. "I've always loved your voice. Even when you were little and John Kendall would have you do some mundane job in the barn to keep you busy. I would stop outside to listen to you sing." He stepped closer as he laid his hand on her cheek, and her breath caught while his deep voice vibrated through her. "I've seen you in concert twice in Dallas. You were even more amazing tonight."

Holy hell, he was going to kiss her! She turned away before either of them could act on the incredible magnetism drawing them to each other.

As if to get himself under control, he took a deep breath. She had to dial this attraction back a little. He said he wanted to be her friend and she could talk to him. How could she remind him that was all they could be? Remembering his rush to get out of Gatlin's and his ashen pallor, she asked, "What happened back at the honky-tonk? And don't tell me it was nothing. You acted like a demon was chasing us."

He swiped a hand through his wheat-colored hair and turned toward a shelf holding framed photos. Most of them were of his little boy. She hadn't missed the fact there weren't any of his dead wife.

"I don't like crowds. When they start to get too close I'm reminded of my last mission."

Her father telling her about EJ being involved with a hostage crisis in Jerusalem came to mind. "You have flashbacks?"

He snapped his gaze to her. "Not as much anymore, but they still happen."

She swallowed and leaned against the shelves. "I had nightmares for about two years after Mike tried to kidnap me and shot my dad. One of my counselors said I had PTSD."

He snorted and rubbed the back of his neck. "I know I did."

"Want to talk about it?"

He shifted to stand in front of her, effectively blocking her escape. "No."

Before she could comprehend what was happening, his lips settled over hers. She gasped, and he took the opening she provided to sweep his tongue into her mouth. He tasted of coffee and hot, sweet man. She wanted him, but needed to fight him. When he suckled on her bottom lip, she couldn't find the strength to deny her desire. She dueled with his tongue and snaked her hands round his waist while he held her head between his warm, strong hands and deepened the kiss to toe-curling hot.

* * * *

EJ pulled out of their sensual kiss lightheaded and wanting much more. His breathing came hard, and his senses filled with her fragrance of soft lilac and lilies. He held her face between his hands and stared into the deep jade pools of her eyes, but instead the passion they'd shared reflected in them, sorrow shined back at him.

Damn, what had he done?

He took a breath and stepped away from her. "I'm sorry. I shouldn't have done that."

She touched his arm, and he turned to meet her haunted gaze. "EJ, I can't be more than your friend."

Did she still love the rock star? He ran his hand through his hair and put some distance between them. Fuck, what did he care if she was in love with someone else? She was pregnant with another man's baby. He couldn't let himself feel anything for her. She'd end up hurting him like his wife had.

"I'm pregnant and it wouldn't be fair to you or my baby to get involved with anyone."

Her words twisted his insides. "Do you still love the father?"

She shook her head and let out a short bitter laugh. "Fabian? I'm not sure I ever loved him. I was infatuated early on, and then he became as much of a bad habit as coke and booze did, but I can't let my baby pay for my stupidity. As for Fabian, he wants nothing to do with us."

Defeat numbed his limbs, even as relief flooded him. He couldn't let himself fall for her. She would cause him pain, but he wanted her. Friendship wasn't, nor would it ever be, enough. "When are you going to let the world know about the baby? You won't be able to hide it much longer under baggy t-shirts and high waists."

She faced the CDs again. "I'm not sure what I'm going to do. But I'm not ready for anyone to know about it."

Her words sliced through him. The memory of Raquel telling him about her pregnancy oddly echoed Emily's words. *"Oh, EJ, I'm pregnant. What are we going to do? No one can know about it yet."*

"I think I should take you home."

His tone came out harsher than he'd wanted it to, but he didn't apologize for it.

"No. I'll call Momma." She headed to the front door, where she turned and looked back. "See you around."

With that she was gone, leaving him with a strange pain in his heart.

Chapter 10

Two weeks had passed since the kiss.

Two weeks of thinking about a man who'd turned her inside out and upside down.

Why had EJ become gruff with her after Emily told him they couldn't be more than friends? Maybe she'd misread him. He may not have wanted the happily ever after. Had he simply wanted them to be friends with benefits? The questions swirled around in her mind like mist over the Tennessee mountains. Elusive, slippery, and impossible to grasp. But one thing remained. After reconnecting with him and the friendship they'd once had, she missed him.

She hadn't seen him since that night. Last weekend, his family had been invited to celebrate her dad's birthday, but EJ declined saying he had to work. Tucker, Vince, and their families had come to the backyard party. They'd brought along EJ's little boy, and she loved playing with Austin. He could easily steal her heart as quickly as his father could, if she'd let them.

Today was EJ's thirtieth birthday party. She'd been anxious about it for a week now, and didn't know what she'd get him. But soon she had the perfect inspiration and got busy on his birthday present.

Turning around as she inspected her reflection in the mirror, she smiled. She looked as hot as the summer sun in the sundress she'd chosen with help from her mother. Momma had been right. It was perfect. With its low cut corset styling and delicate embroidery, the eye was drawn to the top of the dress and not to the slight bulge of her lower belly hidden beneath the full short skirt. She stepped into the high-heeled sandals, again with the hope people would look at her long legs and not at her midsection and the baby she soon wouldn't be able to hide.

A knock sounded at her door. "Emily, we're leaving," her mother said before opening the door to peek in. "You sure you don't want to come with us?"

"No, I'd like to have my own car in case I need to leave." She wanted a way to escape, not only the temptation of the alcohol flowing freely, but also EJ if things got too uncomfortable with him.

"Okay. See you there." Momma smiled and closed the door.

Emily turned to her dresser to apply her makeup. She didn't wear much--a bit of shadow, eyeliner and mascara to make her eyes pop, and bright berry-colored lipstick.

Her cell buzzed, and she picked it up off the edge of the dresser. Glancing at the ID, she hit the button to answer. Before she could speak, her assistant's frantic voice shattered her good humor. "He's out of jail."

"Kelly? What are you talking about?" Emily sat on the edge of her bed as dread filled her. She only knew one person who was in jail.

"Your stepfather." Kelly's voice shook with her fear. "He called me looking for you."

"What did he want?" Her stomach plummeted to her feet at the prospect of Mike Ritter being out of jail. But how? He'd been sentenced to life in prison, and he wouldn't be up for parole for at least another fifteen to twenty years.

"I don't know. He told me he's out and coming for you." Her voice became shrill as she spoke. "God, Emily, I'm scared for you. He sounded absolutely crazy."

"How did he find your number?" Emily's heart raced as cold fear numbed her limbs.

"He called me on the business phone. I figured it was another tabloid reporter. But it was him."

Kelly had been fielding all of her PR calls for months and keeping Emily's whereabouts completely out of the tabloids. The world thought she was holed up in Nashville, which was exactly what she wanted them to think. Kelly's business cell was the only phone number connected to her. All the other numbers associated with her, including her parents' and Mike's parents' cells and home phones were private numbers. "Kelly, listen to me. Get rid of the business cell and call Trish. You both have to stay safe. Lord knows what he will do."

"I will. What are you going to do?"

Emily stared at her reflection in the mirror above the dresser as her world spun out of control. "I don't know."

* * * *

EJ read the APB from the Texas Justice Department for what had to have been the hundredth time, and his heart sank to his belly a little farther.

Franklin Michael Ritter III (aka Michael Ritter and Mike Ritter) escaped a work detail today at 1300 CST outside the Clements Unit of the Texas Department of Justice, Amarillo. He is believed to be heading to McAllister, Texas, and should be considered armed and dangerous.

He needed to leave the office. His family had planned a birthday party for him at Tucker's ranch, but first, he had to warn Mike's family and the Kendalls he might come looking for them. After finding the phone number for Mike's second ex-wife, he called Tammy Jo McAllister. She lived in the mansion her father had built at the edge of town with her eight-year-old son. Although EJ didn't believe Mike would come after the heiress to the town's founding family, he couldn't take that chance. As far as he knew, she'd denied any contact between Mike and his son from the day of his birth. Even legally changed the boy's name to McAllister after Mike's conviction.

The call went as predicted. Tammy Jo took the threat seriously and would hire more security to protect her and her son. Next, he called Mike's parents. They assured EJ they would call if Mike contacted them and would let their ranch hands know to stay watchful. They'd call Mary Jane, Mike's sister, who lived in Dallas with her husband, and warn her as well. He hung up the phone and looked to the door where Deputy Clint Grier leaned against the doorframe.

Clint had been a deputy under Mike when he'd been sheriff and was the lead singer of the band Lawman. He'd been Mike's arresting officer when he'd shot Seth Kendall after a local concert at the fairgrounds. "I saw the APB."

EJ nodded and leaned back in his seat. "Do you think he's stupid enough to show up here?"

Clint entered the office and sat in the chair in front of EJ's desk. "I do. He swore he'd punish those who'd put him in jail. He especially has it out for Emily. Abby showed me a letter he'd sent to Emily after he was convicted." The older man shook his head and rubbed along his square jaw. "He threatened she'd never be safe. The moment he got out of jail he would find her and kill her. He's one sick son of a bitch."

Emily had mentioned the letter and her memory of Mike's confession at the trial the other night. Did she know how dangerous he was? "Damn." He stood and reached for his hat on the rack by the desk. He'd change out of his uniform and head straight over to Tucker's place. "C'mon. I know the Kendalls plan to come to the party. I don't want to give them this news over the phone." Especially to Emily. How would she take it? Would her fear send her back to the crutch drugs and alcohol provided? Or would she let him protect her?

He made his way to the locker room as the seditious voice in his head whispered, *How can you protect her? You couldn't save your team or the dignitaries. Hell, you couldn't even save your own wife from herself.*

* * * *

In a daze, Emily parked in the grass next to the driveway. Following the noise of the party around the house she'd grown up in to the backyard, she hoped the people at the party wouldn't mob her as they had the other night. EJ's sisters approached and gushed about how much they loved her country music.

"I wish you would sing country again," the one with curly blond hair said. The other one wore her blond locks long and straight. Emily could never tell the sisters apart, she knew their names were Lori and Becky, but that was about it.

She gave the women a forced smile and fudged the truth. "I have something in the works. Please, excuse me. I have to find my parents."

At the edge of the rows of tables set up in the backyard under a large tent, she studied the faces of family friends and neighbors until she found EJ and Clint Grier talking to her mom and dad under a tree at the edge of the yard. EJ glanced at her, and by the seriousness shining in his expression, her heart fell. Kelly had been right. Mike was out of jail.

She joined her parents and her father instantly wrapped his arm around her shoulders. "We got some bad news."

"I know." Emily swallowed and snaked her arm around her dad's waist. In her other hand she held the small wrapped gift she'd brought for EJ. "Mike contacted my assistant in Nashville and told her he was coming after me. He must have found my business number on the Internet. As far as I know, the media still thinks I'm in Nashville. How did he get out of prison?"

"All we know from the APB is he escaped from work release and he may be headed here." EJ shifted his stance, narrowing his brows as he met her gaze. "You confirmed you are his main target. He might not be on his way here at all, but Nashville." He turned to Clint. "Call the FBI to let them know this new development."

Clint nodded and headed toward the front of the house.

"What do you suggest we do?" Momma asked. "Seth is leaving Monday to go on tour."

Dad's stormy green eyes narrowed. "I'll cancel the tour."

"Actually, it might be better if you left. Take Abby, Emily, and your little boy with you."

Johnny let out a giggle as he chased two of the Cowley kids around a sprinkler set up nearby. What would Mike do to her little brother if he ever got his hands on him? Before either Dad or Momma could reject the idea, Emily said, "That's perfect. Y'all get out of town. If no one is in McAllister for Mike to bother with, he'll stay out of town."

She knew how unlikely Mike forgetting about the town was, but she had to protect her family.

"You're coming with us." Her mother's voice shook.

"No, Momma, I can't." She looked around to make sure no one was listening and lowered her voice. "I'm going into hiding right here. I'm this close"--she held her thumb and forefinger together--"to showing. I'm not ready for the world to know I'm pregnant."

Her mother's eyes widened as she glanced at EJ.

"Emily told me about the pregnancy." EJ rested his hand on Emily's arm. "Emily, I think you should go with your parents."

Emily glanced at him and took strength in his touch. "I can't. I'm afraid to go on the road again. There are too many temptations, and I'd rather risk Mike finding me here than falling off the wagon."

Her father's shoulders fell as he looked at the ground, then he slowly nodded. If anything would convince them the road was the most dangerous place for her now, it was the fear she could be tempted to use drugs again. "I understand your concern." When his gaze landed on EJ, Emily shivered at the intensity. "Okay, I'll take Abby and Johnny on the road with me, but I'm trusting you to keep my daughter safe."

"I will." EJ fisted his hands at his sides. "I won't let anything to happen to her." He turned to her and his pale blue shirt softened the hue of his eyes. "None of you can go anywhere alone."

Her mother nodded. "We understand."

Dad looked at Emily, concern etching the corners of his eyes. "Do you want to leave?"

She didn't want to go anywhere before she had a chance to talk to EJ. "No. We're here to celebrate EJ's birthday. I can't imagine being anywhere safer."

Dad didn't look convinced, but nodded and moved away with her mother.

"You should go with them."

She faced EJ. "You know why I can't. I truly am afraid of the road, but if I leave, Mike will follow us. I'll never be safe, and neither will my family."

"He'll get caught long before then." EJ pursed his lips, making them even more kissable.

"I'm sure he will. But is it before or after he hurts someone I love?"

He closed his eyes and took a breath. "I see your point. You have no intention of staying hidden here, do you?"

"Nope. I plan to make my stay in town well known. Now, let's forget about Mike Ritter and celebrate you becoming an old man."

He huffed and smirked. "Old…eh?"

She shrugged and held out the gift with a smile. "Happy birthday. I know there's a table for gifts, but I'd rather you open this now."

He took the package. "You didn't have to get me anything."

She shrugged and folded her hands in front of her. "I'm hoping we can still be friends."

"I'd like that." He looked up from the package in his hand. "Especially since it looks like I've appointed myself your protector, and knowing what you have planned, you won't make it an easy job."

Heat flooded her face. "About that. I want to thank you."

His gaze took on a fierce blaze as he brushed his fingers over her cheek, warming her flesh even more. "I won't let anything happen to you."

She took his hand and squeezed it. "I know. Now, go on, open your gift."

He chuckled and ripped the plain pale yellow paper from the plastic case. Upon reading the front of the CD, he snapped his gaze to hers.

Swallowing the sudden lump in her throat, she pointed to it. "I made it for you in Dad's recording studio. Most of the songs have never been recorded before and are simple arrangements of me and my guitar or a piano. There isn't anything fancy."

"Thank you. I know I'll love it." His voice rasped and she almost didn't hear him. He took a step toward her and for a split second, she thought he was going to kiss her, and her breath caught with the sudden desire for his lips to be on hers. She wasn't sure if she was more relieved or disappointed when he smiled and held the case to his chest. "This is the best gift I could ever get."

From the deck looking over the backyard, Tucker announced they would be serving dinner and everyone should choose their seats. She turned to head toward her parents' table. He took her hand, stopping her.

"Join me?"

At the thought of spending all evening with him, heat warmed her clear through. "Are you asking me to be your date at your own party?"

With a chuckle, he shrugged. "I suppose I am."

The excitement of spending time with him warred with the need to keep him at arm's length. "EJ, I can't be more than your friend."

"I know." A shadow passed over his eyes as he nodded. "That's all I want, too."

* * * *

EJ let go of her hand and led her to where the rest of his family sat at a long table in the front of the tent. Even his parents, aunt, and uncle had come from Arizona for his party. He introduced her to them. They graciously ignored her superstardom and talked about when she was a little girl.

He took Austin out of his mother's arms and turned him to Emily.

She smiled brightly and took the little boy's hand when he held it out to her. "Hello again, Austin."

"Hi." Austin giggled, then hid his face in his father's chest.

"Since when are you ever shy?" EJ shook his head. "He likes you."

"We had fun at Dad's party last weekend." She met EJ's gaze, and the flame he'd seen in her eyes blazed hot enough to boil his blood. She might be fighting her attraction to him, but it was there.

He wanted her, and despite all of her standoffishness, she wanted him as badly. Could he only be her friend and now her protector? But how could he ever be more? She was the wrong woman for him, he knew that. What if she went back to using drugs? What about the baby? Maybe the reason for the secrecy was because she didn't want it.

He put Austin in the highchair beside him and pulled out the seat on the other side of him for Emily to sit. A moment later, they headed to the buffet table filled with dishes holding grilled hamburgers, hotdogs, barbecue, potato salad, and corn on the cob. As they ate the delicious food, she charmed his family with stories of how EJ had teased her as a girl on the ranch.

After they'd finished the meal with chocolate cake, Emily excused herself, asking Judy if she may use the bathroom. EJ watched her weave her way through the tables and head into the house.

"You fancy her."

Blinking, he met his dad's solemn expression. "Emily is my friend."

"You need to make sure that's all." His mother set her glass of sweet tea on the table and folded her knobby hands before her. "I've read some terrible things about her. You've been hurt once by a woman like her. You don't need that again. Think about what it would do to Austin."

They didn't have to tell him twice. "I know. Now, will you please drop it?"

After several minutes, EJ began to wonder where Emily was. The DJ, who'd been playing a steady stream of country music from the deck, stopped an old George Strait tune mid-song. Emily sat on a stool in the center of the deck and tapped the microphone the DJ handed her. After a ping sounded over the sound system, she put it in the cradle on the mic stand the DJ set before her and shifted her signature guitar in her lap. "Hi, y'all."

When the people gathered applauded, she held up a hand. "We came here tonight to honor a good man." She met EJ's gaze and smiled as the group turned and clapped their hands or whistled toward him.

He held up his hand and nodded his head once to acknowledge his friends and family. What was she doing?

"I've known EJ Cowley almost my whole life. When I was about ten, my cat Misty died. I was devastated until EJ came over to my house with the cutest golden tabby kitten I'd ever seen. For the next eleven years, Goldie was one of my very best friends."

The people around him looked at him and smiled, saying, "Ahh" and "Oh wasn't that sweet."

His attention was fully on the woman on stage. A breeze ruffled her hair, and she ran her hand through the short strands to settle them off her face. "Sadly, Goldie passed away a little over a year ago."

The statement brought a round of condolences from her audience. Tucker called out, "Since he's nice, he should give you another one."

As the party goers yelled out their agreement to the statement, Emily smiled. "Oh, don't let EJ's sweetness make you think he didn't torment the heck out of me at times, too." Several people chuckled, and she went on, "One time we went fishing with my grandfather and his dad. EJ thought it would be hilarious to put a frog down my shirt, knowing I hate anything slimy and gross. Remember that, EJ?"

He nodded and snickered. God, she was turning his world upside down. "I do. You let out a squeal to rival a war cry."

The family and friends gathered laughed. She never looked more radiant as she winked at him. "I wrote this song for a man I'm quickly considering one of my best friends."

Emily ensnared him as she played a sweet melody on her guitar then added a voice certainly blessed by the angels.

She sang about the times they'd spent together riding horseback over the ranch and of fishing in the river. About him giving her a kitten and the incident with the frog. She was the girl with long pigtails, and he was the boy who liked to tug on them. The song ended talking about a friendship that would never end.

By the time she was finished, he was totally under her spell.

He was falling for a woman he could never risk more than being friends with.

* * * *

Emily set her guitar in its case inside the dining area of the kitchen when she sensed someone behind her.

"You and EJ, uh?"

The voice startled her, and she spun around. As her heart returned to its regular speed, she grinned. "Trevor Marshall?"

The man standing in front of her nodded and smiled. Trevor had spiked dark hair, and was dressed in black jeans and a pale yellow shirt with the top button open. His style had always been different. While they were in middle school, they were best friends. He'd been the one who helped her through her mother's divorce with Mike and his marriage to a woman she hadn't liked. She'd leaned on him during the turbulent time of learning Seth Kendall was her biological father and Mike was a criminal. She helped him through his troubled teens when he discovered he had no attraction to girls. Most people, including his parents, had thought they were more than friends, but she knew the truth. Trevor was gay. He wrapped her up into a hug and held her for a moment. When he pulled back, he said, "How are you?"

"I'm good. What are you up to these days?" She ignored his first implied question and skipped the truth. She was anything but okay. Her nerves were shot with everything going on: The news of Mike being free, the attraction refusing to let her and EJ be nothing more than friends, the way everyone danced around her recent scandals. Even being in the house she'd grown up in was adding to her feeling of being trapped. Although Tucker Cowley and his wife had redecorated the ranch house and made it their own, she couldn't help the flood of memories of times when she was little. Of Mike reading her bedtime stories, of him tucking her in, and telling her he loved her, of his leaving her mother when she was twelve to marry another woman.

What she wouldn't do for a drink and the sweet oblivion she got from coke. The cravings had come upon her before, but nothing like this, and they reminded her that addiction and getting well would take more than coming home or staying away from the road.

"I'm in law school at Stanford University." Trevor squared his shoulders and grinned.

"That's wonderful. You home for the summer?"

He shifted his feet, his self-pride from a moment ago visibly deflating. "Yeah. Mom insists I come home." With a scowl, he looked around the kitchen. "I'd rather stay in California." He lifted a gold chain out of his shirt and looked at the gold circle at the end. "I miss Keith."

She stared at the simple band for a moment. "You're married?" A smile brightened his expression and he nodded. Truly happy for him, she matched his grin and hugged him. "Congratulations!"

As they separated, he said, "Thanks. No one else knows he's not my roommate."

Trevor shouldn't feel ashamed or hide his life from his parents. Someday, he would break free of his mother's control of him. Her life was one fucked-up mess, but she didn't envy the Marshall children. No wonder Raquel ended up committing suicide, despite being married to one of the most wonderful men she knew. Although, Trevor divulged his secret, she wasn't ready to tell him hers. "I'm happy for you. Your secret is safe with me."

She picked up her case. "We'll have to get together sometime."

He nodded and shoved his hands into his pockets. "It was good seeing you again, Emily. I'm glad you came home."

"Me too." The need to escape and get away from the people outside become too much. She patted him on his arm with her other hand, which she couldn't keep from shaking. "See you around, Trevor."

She was halfway to the front door when EJ caught up with her. "You shouldn't go anywhere alone."

No, she shouldn't and not because her psycho stepfather wanted her dead. With a deep sigh, she nodded. "I know. I need to get away from everyone."

"Okay." He studied her face as if he could see every one of her secrets and took the case from her, then led her out side. Once he secured the guitar in the trunk, he leaned against the frame of her car. "Thank you for the performance. I think it made everyone's evening. Including mine."

She stopped pacing. He grinned at her and the pull toward him overwhelmed her. The desire coursing through her for him was as demanding as the craving for coke. He could easily become her distraction from the irritating addiction, but she wouldn't use him.

"I'm glad. There are times when I wish I knew more than music."

"How are the plans for the record company coming?" He shifted his feet and shoved his hands into his jeans pockets.

"We have a tentative name: Kendall McKenna Records." Emily leaned against the back of her car beside him. "Our lawyers are writing up the contracts and taking care of all the other crap. I don't understand all of the business end of it." She shook her head and forced a smile suddenly feeling very much alone. "I'll admit I never dreamed I'd have a partnership in a business. My ignorance about all of this stuff makes me feel stupid."

"You aren't stupid. None of us know everything. You know more than most people do about the music business. Hell, I don't know anything about it. If you want to learn more, you could always take classes."

She folded her arms over her chest. "I don't know. I never thought about going to college and have no real desire to go now. I wasn't a bad student, but I hated school. Mike used to get mad at me because I didn't care about getting As. All he talked about before the shit went down with him was me going to college. All I ever wanted to do was sing." She let out a bitter snort as she thought of Trevor Marshall and the law degree he'd someday have. "You know Glenda Marshall was right. If there had been romantic feelings between me and Trevor, I would've ruined him eventually." With a shake of her head, she walked past him. "I guess I'll go around back. Maybe Dad can take me home. I can't be alone, but I can't stay here."

EJ's gentle touch on her arm stopped her, then he took her hand. "C'mon, let's take a walk."

"I can't let you leave your own party." She bit her lip and shook her head. "Besides, what about Austin?"

"No one will miss me. Austin is being spoiled rotten by his grandparents." He quirked his head toward the barn and dark pasture. "No more excuses."

"Okay."

He led her past the parked vehicles crowding the driveway to the corral near the barn. She paused when he stepped onto the grassy, rutted path made by the ATVs Tucker used to carry hay to his stock. EJ looked back at her, then glanced at her feet. "Guess we can't go too far without you breaking your neck in those crazy shoes."

She glanced down at the platform wedges. "Not that way anyway." With a wink, she slipped out of the shoes and picked them up. Holding the designer heels by their back straps with her index finger, she grinned. "But I can always take them off."

With a shake of his head, he wrapped an arm around her back and guided her along the fence. "C'mon then. We won't go far, but I want us to be able to talk."

When they reached the back of the barn, he opened the door and they went inside. He turned on the fluorescent lights, and she looked around. Unlike the interior of the house, not much of the barn had changed from when she was a little girl. Four horses nickered at the interruption in their sleep and peered over their stall doors at Emily and EJ. She wished she had some horse cookies to treat them with.

He wrapped his arm around her waist and held her close. "What exactly do you have planned regarding Mike?"

She shrugged and snaked her hand around him. His warmth seeped through his shirt into her, adding fuel to her out of control desire and heated the icy places caused by her addiction. "I'm going to have my assistant call the tabloids to let them know I'm here."

He stiffened and furrowed his brows. "Won't that put a target on your back for every hack with a camera?"

And hopefully for Mike to find me, too. "Probably."

"I don't like it." As he spoke, he pulled her tighter into his embrace. His breath warmed her ear as he spoke in a deep timbre. "You're taking a huge risk. I don't want you staying at the Double K alone."

"I won't be. Vince and the other ranch hands live nearby." As she caressed his back, her breathing quickened. "Besides, I can call in my bodyguards."

He pulled away enough to meet her gaze. "That isn't good enough. If I'm going to keep you safe, I need to be under the same roof as you."

Her heart stuttered over a beat. "What do you mean?"

"When your parents leave on Monday, I want you to move into my house."

Shaking her head, she stepped away from him. Despite the warm evening, a chill ran down her back. Her belly quivered at the thought of being close to him and yet having to stay far away. "EJ, I can't move in with you. Dear God, it would only be a matter of time before some tabloid reporter discovered I'm living with you. Do you have any idea how that would affect you--us?"

He stepped in front of her and feathered his fingers over her cheek to her temple. "I don't care about anything except keeping you safe. Either you move into my house or I stay at the Double K."

She had to make him see reason. "What about Austin? If I'm with you, he will be in danger, too."

His jaw twitched as if he clenched his teeth. Good, she'd hit a chord with him.

He lost the pensive expression and lifted one side of his mouth. "I'll ask my mom and dad to take him back to Arizona. They would love to have him for a few weeks."

"EJ, this isn't going to--"

He leaned forward and placed his lips over hers, effectively stopping the flow of words. She opened under him, and he deepened the kiss. He tasted sweet and intoxicating as he caressed her mouth. Dropping her shoes behind him, she pulled him close and gave as good as she got. She could easily fall for this amazing man, but she couldn't let their flirtations, his goodness, and his strength get to her heart. No matter how much she wanted him.

He pulled out of the kiss and rested his forehead on hers, his breaths coming as hard and fast as hers. "I know we can't be more than friends, Emily. But I have to warn you. I don't think I can stay away from you."

His words caused the hair on her arms to stand on end and her knees weakened. She was losing the battle between her desire for him and her good sense telling her to stay way. Could she have the type of relationship he was suggesting?

Was it possible to keep her heart protected from him if they complicated their friendship with sex?

She honestly didn't know, but damn it, she wanted him too much not to explore the possibilities.

Unable to deny her need, she captured his lips again as she threaded her fingers into his hair, knocking his hat off to fall to the hay-littered floor with her shoes. She delved into his mouth and explored the sweet depths. He groaned and pulled her tighter against him. Wanting to get as close as possible, she lifted her leg to hook over his hip, which brought his erection right where she wanted it. He caressed his hand from her waist to the bare thigh exposed under her dress. When he touched her damp panties, she moaned and moved against his hand.

With a growl, he broke the kiss. "Emily, we have to stop. Damn, I want you."

"I know." She struggled to catch her breath and let her leg slide to the ground. "We had better get back. Someone might come looking for us."

He picked up his hat and her shoes. As he put his Stetson on, he handed her the sandals. She reached up with her free hand and wiped her finger over his lips. His breath caught at her touch. "You have my lipstick all over you."

With a chuckle, he took her hand and pressed a kiss to her fingers. "I'm sure it will be hard to hide what we've been up to for the past half-hour in the barn." He captured her lips again and kissed her with all the promise of more to come.

"Hey, there you are. Tucker is chopping at the bit to start the fireworks." Vince came through the front door of the breezeway. "Oh… Am I interrupting something?"

EJ pulled away and grinned, but Emily leaned into his chest and laughed hard enough to make tears came to her eyes as a memory of another interrupted kiss flashed in her mind.

He wrapped his arms around her. "Emily, what's wrong. Vince won't tell anyone what he saw."

"Is she crying?" Vince asked with a hint of panic in his voice.

The brothers' assumptions made her peals of laughter sound more like sobs. What was wrong with her? Was it the stress of everything going on causing a breakdown? Sure, the similarity between her current situation and the one she'd walked in on when she was fourteen between her parents was funny, but she was on the verge of hysteria and these two poor men were helpless.

Shaking her head, she looked up into EJ's concerned expression. He used his thumb to wipe tears from her eyes. "I'm sorry. It's--" she gasped for air and control as another giggle bubbled up--"I'm okay. When my dad came back to McAllister, I caught him and my mom kissing in this same barn."

"Is history repeating itself?" EJ chuckled and held her around the waist as they headed out the way Vince had come in.

She shook her head. What did he mean? Was he implying they, too, would end up like her parents? The implication sobered her and sent a shiver through her. "You know it can't."

"Wait." Vince paused beside them. "Are you two dating?"

"No," both Emily and EJ said at the same time as they stared at each other.

At least he understood the truth. They probably would end up in bed, and soon if the intensity of their kisses were any indication, but they couldn't ever have more than what they had now. Love could never enter into the equation.

God help her, she could fall in love with him.

"C'mon, Vince." He slapped his brother on the shoulder. "Stop trying to figure it out. You're already crazy enough."

Chapter 11

EJ entered his kitchen from feeding his three horses and making sure the twenty cattle had hay. Someday he wanted to work the five hundred acre ranch to its full potential, but that would have to wait until he stopped needing a day job to make ends meet.

He sensed his mother's probing stare as he hung his hat on the rack by the door and slipped out of his barn boots. Sleep hadn't come easy to EJ, and he didn't want to deal with his mother's questions at six-thirty on a Sunday morning. He'd spent the restless night listening to the CD Emily had given him and being seduced by the sexiest voice he'd ever heard. By morning, he had a hard-on he needed an icy shower to take care of. He knew without a doubt he would have sex with Emily Kendall sooner rather than later.

His mother made two mugs of coffee using his Keurig and set them on the table. As she sat in one of the chairs, she said, "Come. Sit. We have to talk about Austin."

Following Tucker's impressive fireworks show--the legality of which EJ didn't want to investigate--he'd asked his parents if they would take Austin with them when they returned to Arizona. He hadn't provided a reason for the visit. But if his mother's imposing presence was any indication, he'd have to give her one now.

He swallowed and pulled out the chair opposite her.

After he sat, she squared her shoulders and leaned over her arms resting on the table. Although he and his brothers all towered over Meredith Cowley, no one questioned her authority. Even his father bowed to her when she turned her no-bullshit blue-eyed stare on him. Like the one she gave him now. "There has to be something going on with you if you're willing to face Glenda Marshall's wrath by letting us take Austin home with us. Don't give me a pack of lies either. I saw how you looked at the Kendall girl last night. Then you disappeared with her after she put on that performance. I saw the CD she gave you. How serious are the two of you?"

"Mom, I told you we're friends." His mother didn't need to know about his wanting *benefits* with their friendship. "That's all."

She sipped her coffee as she regarded him with sharp scrutiny. He couldn't help but squirm in his chair. Damn, the woman wasn't going to let any of this go.

"Is her baby yours?" She set her mug on the table.

He blinked. Too shocked that she figured out Emily's secret and thought the baby was his to do much but open his mouth then close it again. Finally he sputtered, "What?

She leaned back, pursed her lips, and shook her head. "You didn't know she's pregnant. Figures. Men are dense. She hides it well, but a girl as tall and naturally slender as she is doesn't have a belly, unless she's got a baby in there."

"I know she's pregnant." He picked up the creamer and poured a generous amount into his coffee. As he sipped it, he wished for something a hell of a lot stronger than Folgers. "The baby isn't mine. It belongs to her ex-husband. Please keep quiet about it. She doesn't want it to become public knowledge yet." If his mother knew about the baby, others surely did too. He'd have to warn Emily.

His mother narrowed her eyes. "Edward James, what's going on? You aren't sending Austin with us while you have fun with some woman, are you? I know you've always had a bond with her, but she isn't the same girl. If she's pregnant with another man's baby, then there's even more reason to stay clear."

"Mom, nothing happened between Emily and me. Nothing will," he outright lied. The thought of their kisses had him shifting in his seat.

"She may have become a beautiful woman, but fame has damaged her, son," she went on as if she hadn't heard him. Or believed him, more like it. "You need to stay away from her."

He'd be lying to himself if the only reason for sending Austin away was to protect him from what Mike Ritter might do. Austin needed protection from looking at Emily as a potential mommy. When the craziness going on between him and Emily was over, Austin would be spared a broken heart.

What about you?

EJ refused to consider the answer.

"I would be lying if I said I wasn't attracted to her, but we are *just* friends." He ignored the skeptical twist to his mother's mouth. "I'm sending Austin with you to keep him safe. Mike Ritter escaped from prison yesterday, and he's gunning for Emily. Seth is going out on tour and taking Abby and their little boy with him, but Emily is staying here." Leaning over the table, he cupped his hands around his mug. The warmth seeped into his suddenly cold palms.

"Why isn't she going with them?"

"She's afraid of the temptations of the road."

"Because she's a drug addict." His mother clucked her tongue. "Another reason not to get involved with her problems. I realize you're a grown man and have needs only a woman can fulfill, but I don't ever want to see you in the mess of hurt you were in when Raquel died."

"*Mom*." He winced at his mother's reference to his sex life. The reminder of why nothing could ever develop between him and Emily pinched his heart uncomfortably. Although accepting her baby as his own would be easy if she'd let him, he couldn't afford to lose his heart to another drug addict. All they could ever have was sex. "Nothing is going on between Emily and me. If you don't want to take Austin home, I'll ask Glenda to keep him for a few weeks. I need devote time to protecting Emily from a dangerous man. Austin would be safer away from here."

"We'll take Austin, but protecting her shouldn't be your job."

He picked up his cup and drained it. "I'm the sheriff. So, yes, it is my job. Now, may we please drop this?"

His mother flattened her lips into a displeased line and stood. She rested a hand bent with arthritis on his shoulder, surprising him with her strength as she squeezed. "I'm worried about you, son. You've been through enough pain."

* * * *

On Monday morning, Emily stood on the porch, drained her second cup of tea, and watched the gray clouds swirling in the south western sky. Severe weather was in the forecast, which added to her unease.

"I should cancel the tour."

She looked over her shoulder at her father standing next to her scowling at the sky. "Dad, we've been over this a hundred times. You can't cancel the tour."

The furrow in his brow deepened and his jaw twitched as if he clenched his teeth. "I don't care about anything but keeping you safe."

"EJ will keep me safe. We've been over the plan. You even agreed it was a good one. Besides, Mike could be caught by the police long before he comes to McAllister." After his parents, Austin, his aunt, and uncle left for the airport, EJ had come over to the Double K and outlined how he'd protect Emily. He'd let out her plan to go public with her whereabouts, but his ideas would work despite her practically inviting her deranged stepfather to come and get her.

She would move to his ranch. During this time, EJ would work from home as much as he could, and when he had to go into town, one of his most senior deputies would stay at the ranch. Emily also contacted her two bodyguards. They were flying in from Nashville today and would be here by evening. Oliver and Jason would take turns guarding her twenty-four/seven.

The thought of living in the same house with EJ had her nerves more rattled than the bad weather and Mike's threat rolled into one. Then again, maybe all of the worry was for nothing. Mike could be caught. Reports of his escape were on every news outlet in the country, while law enforcement agencies in five states and the FBI were looking for him. He'd have to stop for food or gas sometime. Hopefully that would be when he got captured.

"About EJ, what's going on with the two of you?" Dad sipped his coffee. "I'm glad if something is there. He's a good man."

She filled her lungs with the humid air of the pending storm and turned to her father. Damn, sometime she hated her decision to embrace total truth. "In all honesty, we're playing with fire."

"What does that mean?" Her father's puzzled expression would have been funny under other circumstances. Sometimes he still thought of her as the fourteen-year-old girl he'd first met eight years ago.

She shrugged and set her cup on the porch railing, wishing for more tea. "We're attracted to each other, and we've…eh… kissed a few times. Nothing can come of it. I'm pregnant with another man's child." EJ was the kind of man she would have loved to be her baby's father, but she could wish all she wanted, it would never be true. At the thought, her heart constricted painfully. "Considering I was brought up in a similar situation, I won't let another man take on being father to my daughter. Despite my wish that he'll stay away, I know someday Fabian will be back. He'll realize what he's missed out on and…"

At the way his face pinched, she looked out over the front yard. "I'm sorry, Daddy."

He leaned against the porch post and rubbed a hand over his chest as if it hurt. Maybe it did, and she wished she could take the words she'd said back.

"No, you're right," he said in such a deep voice, the words trembled over her like a bass drum. "Mike may have been the catalyst that caused your mother to marry him and trick me into staying away. But I didn't fight for you. I should have. It's my biggest regret." He wrapped his arm around her shoulders, pulled her close, and placed a soft kiss on her temple. "I love you, Emily. I always have, but I wasn't here when I should have been."

She swallowed the sudden lump of old pain rubbed raw by all the things going on in her life now. The one question she'd always wondered about yanked on her conscious like a trout on a string. She'd never been brave enough to ask it. Despite not knowing if she wanted it answered, she had to ask. She looked over her shoulder and met his gaze. His green eyes, copies of her own, filled with pain, regret, and a storm of other emotions.

Her mouth was as dry as the West Texas desert, and her voice box constricted. She had to ask the question that had plagued her ever since she'd figured out Seth Kendall was her biological father. "Would you have come back if your dad hadn't died?"

The moisture gathering at her father's eyes surprised her and humbled her. He sniffed and blinked, pushing tears from the corners of his eyes. As he brushed his fingers over her cheek, he rasped, "Yes. I would have come back. I may not have come back the day I did, but I planned to come home. I realized what I--"

"Missed," she finished for him--not unkindly, but matter-of-factly-- and turned her face toward the storm.

"Oh, God, Emily, can you ever forgive me?"

Closing her eyes, she thought of the things she had to ask forgiveness for, but she wasn't ready to dig up the agonizing confession. She brushed a stray tear from her cheek and faced him again. "I forgave you a long time ago, Daddy. But it doesn't change the fact I'm pregnant with another little girl who will grow up not knowing her father. Though this time instead of some weird-assed crazy man keeping them apart, it's because he doesn't want her. He's too busy chasing fame and snorting coke."

She kissed his cheek and stepped away. "Now, you had better get on the road or you'll miss your plane."

* * * *

Emily set her purse on the dresser and looked around the bedroom EJ showed her after picking her up from the Double K. Although spare of excess decoration--the only splash of color was the multi-hued patchwork quilt on the full-sized bed--the room was spacious. A heavy oak dresser sat along one wall, while a small desk sat between the windows. Simple sheer curtains obscured the worst of the storm raging outside.

EJ set her suitcase next to the wall and pointed toward a door by the corner. "There's the closet and the bathroom is right next door in the hall." He rubbed his jaw. "Since I use the one attached to my room, you'll have it all to yourself. I hope the room is okay."

She faced him and smiled. "It's perfect. Hopefully I'll only be here for a few days and life can go back to normal." Though what qualified as normal, she had no idea. Two of her bodyguards would take turns guarding the house and live in EJ's empty bunkhouse. Until Mike's capture, she was trapped here. Afterward, she'd have to announce her pregnancy to the world. Hiding it wouldn't be an option any longer. EJ told her his mother guessed about her pregnancy. How many more people suspected her secret? With a shake of her head at the situation, she said, "You seemed surprised by Oliver and Jason."

He folded his arms over his chest. The way his biceps bulged under his uniform shirt distracted her enough to cause her to miss the beginning of his sentence.

"...Dallas. I wanted to see you--"

"I'm sorry, I missed the beginning. The rain on the tin roof is loud." She pointed to the ceiling and winced. "What about Dallas?"

He chuckled and moved toward her. Did he figure out that her inattention had nothing to do with the soft tinny patter of the rain?

At the dresser, he stopped and leaned his backside against it. Only a couple of feet separated them. "I was saying, I remembered them as the security guards from the Dallas show I saw. I wanted to see you afterward and tried to get backstage, but those two brutes wouldn't let me go to you. Nor would they get a message to you."

She stared at him. "You tried to see me after one of my shows? Which one? The guys have been with me for over five years since Dad hired them when I started touring on my own. Oliver and Jason even stuck with me when Fabian fired them. They worked for free for a week until I realized what was going on."

"Christmas twenty-sixteen." He took a deep breath and looked down at his hands. "I thought you were the most beautiful woman in the world."

Before Fabian and Raquel. She closed her eyes and faced the windows as she rubbed the goose bumps on her arms. His confession echoed through her mind. Would things have been different if he had been able to see her? Fate was one cold-hearted bitch.

"I was getting threatening letters then. No one was allowed to see me unless they'd been preauthorized." She turned and wrapped her arms around herself as ice filled her veins with regret and anger. Back then she still had a crush on EJ. She would have loved to have seen him, and if he had thought of her as a woman, maybe... She squashed the thought in its tracks. Wishing was for fools. "I've often wondered if the letters were from Mike trying to scare me. Nothing ever came from the threats."

The regret and longing in EJ's gaze mirrored the emotions in her heart. A rumble of thunder broke through their trance, causing her to startle.

She shook her head to clear it. "Do you have any news about Mike?"

He shoved his hands into the pockets of his tan uniform pants. "There was a possible sighting of Mike in a convenience store outside of Nashville this morning, but he disappeared again. He may have a woman with him. His work release detailed him to an Amarillo community center. Apparently, he conned the manager of the center and her daughter into believing him innocent. He was having a sexual affair with the younger woman. The manager is in custody, but the daughter, Brooklyn Jensen, disappeared with Mike. Ms Jensen also worked as a computer technician at the prison, and was responsible for maintaining the ankle monitors the prisoners wore."

"I don't understand how he could have walked away from a work detail." Emily paced from the bed to the desk and back again. "Aren't the prisoners under guard?"

"Mike had on a monitoring device." EJ ran his hand through his hair, mussing the wheat-colored strands. "He was considered a model prisoner, and despite his crimes, he had a lot of freedom within the prison. That's how he got work release to begin with. Ms Jensen's mother said he'd worked at her center for about fifteen months. He'd first met Ms Jensen at the prison when he'd been detailed to the prison's IT department. The FBI figures this is where he started planning his escape."

"By seducing this woman with his sweet talk." When he nodded, she rubbed her arms. In spite of the warm temperature, a chill numbed her to the bone. "Did the prison know about the relationship between Jensen and the center manager?"

"No, they didn't, but the mother was in on the gig."

The whole thing was crazy. "How did Mike get away if he had on one of those bracelets? Fabian had one once when he was under house arrest for a drunk driving offense. He couldn't go anywhere without the thing alerting the authorities."

"According to the manager, her daughter had done something to make Mike's ankle bracelet malfunction several times." EJ folded his arms in front of him and shifted his weight. "When the prison officials would show up, it would be working again and considered a fluke. He'd gone through three of the monitors during his fifteen months. Ms Jensen reported to the prison that his body chemistry somehow messed with the electronics. The last time it *malfunctioned*, the guards weren't as fast to show up, thinking it was another glitch, but this time he'd escaped."

Icy fear settled in her belly as she fell to the edge of the bed. "Dear God, he sounds like a psychopath." She wrapped her arms around herself. "I have to contact Kelly and Trish. He might go after one of them thinking they will lead him to me." At least her parents weren't going to Nashville. They were heading to her dad's first concert in Atlanta, Georgia. "I have to let the world know where I am."

EJ stepped toward her and pulled her up into an embrace. She wrapped her arms around him, grateful for his warmth and strength.

"I wish you didn't feel like you had to paint a target on yourself," he said into her hair.

She pulled away far enough to meet his gaze. "I wish I didn't either. But I don't see any other way. I don't want anyone else to be in danger and hope he's caught long before he gets to me. I have my baby to worry about."

He narrowed his eyes and his hard regard made her uneasy. "You didn't go with your parents because you're afraid of the temptations of drugs and alcohol but because you want to bait Mike."

She stepped back, but he held onto her arms. "I thought you'd figured that out at your party."

"No, I didn't. I knew you wanted the world to know you were here, but I thought you'd stay hidden." His jaw twitched as he clenched his teeth. "Damn it, Emily, this isn't a game. Was any of what you told me and your parents true?"

Emily didn't appreciate his anger, but she understood it. He was responsible for keeping her safe, a job he took seriously. "I didn't totally lie. I'm past the point of hiding my pregnancy and the road would be tough, but I would've gone if it meant keeping my family safe. I would have dealt with the pregnancy news and fought through the temptations. I've been having cravings and haven't fallen off the wagon. I'll never touch drugs or alcohol again. But going with them wouldn't have kept them safe." She moved out of his grasp. Fear made her knees tremble, and she sat on the bed again, facing the windows. Lightning lit up the sky and thunder boomed as the lights flickered in the room. "Here we can predict Mike's movements and control them. If he's been planning his escape for what must have been years, he's too smart to get caught by chance." She met his gaze and prayed she'd never have to face the sick man she once loved as a father. "We have to be smarter than him. I'll be the bait, while you spring the trap. It's the only way to catch him."

Chapter 12

Awed by her strength and her trust that he'd protect her, EJ knelt before her. She placed too much faith in him. But he hadn't done anything to discourage her, had he? Even now, instead of telling her about his failed mission when he got an American ambassador, her advisor, and five members of his Army Ranger team killed, he sat tight-lipped. He should tell her this plan of hers was crazy. However, he couldn't. She was right. Mike was too smart to get caught randomly, and if he was a betting man, EJ would wager the Jensen women weren't his only accomplices. Not all of Mike's organized crime associates had been arrested eight years ago.

For fifteen years, Mike Ritter ran a sex slavery operation out of a cabin on his parents' ranch. He oversaw a local branch of a complex organization of criminals who lured young women out of Mexico and as far south as Central America with empty promises of a better life, then sold them on the black market to the highest bidders. Right under the nose of the sheriff's department he worked for.

The man had tricked a pregnant and scared teenage Abby into marrying him in order to steal her inheritance to set up his part of the operation. When Abby threatened to tell Emily about her real father and to let the world know, he blackmailed her to keep her mouth shut out of fear he'd lose his second wife and all of his lies would explode in his face. Mike Ritter was calculating, ruthless, and extremely dangerous.

EJ caressed the back of his fingers over the satiny skin of her cheek. The combination of her nearness and scent of lilies and lilacs sent his restraint to the limits. "You are an amazing woman."

She gave him a skeptical smile and rested her hands on either side of his face. "Flattery will get you everywhere."

Her fuck-me smoky voice broke his control to hell. As their lips collided in a hot, demanding kiss, he wrapped his arms around her and shifted to lay her on the bed. She threaded her fingers into his hair and held on as their tongues slid together in an erotic mimic of sex. Needing to touch her, he grabbed the bottom of her t-shirt and pulled it up. They broke the kiss long enough for him to pull it over her head. While she made short work of the buttons of his shirt, he hovered above her and drank in the beauty of her full breasts encased in a black lace bra that left little to the imagination.

"God, you're beautiful." He shrugged out of his shirt. "I have condoms if you want me to use them. I haven't been with a woman since Raquel and--"

She placed a finger over his lips to stop his words and shook her head. "I trust you and I'm okay. I was tested for everything under the sun while in rehab"--a smile tugged at the corner of her lips as she rested her hand on the swell of her belly--"and obviously we don't need them for any other reason."

"Good. I hate those things." As he kissed her again, he pushed the waistband of her yoga pants over her hips. She undid his belt, then he left a trail of nipping kisses down her neck to her breasts. When she got his pants open, he shifted off the bed to get rid of the rest of his clothes. She bit her bottom lip as she watched him and removed her own pants, leaving a black thong in place.

After she scooted up the bed to lay her head on the pillows, he climbed back on the mattress and caressed his fingertips down her body from her neck to the roundness of her belly. A lump formed in his throat as he wished the child she carried was his.

She rested her hand over his and met his gaze. "Whatever you're thinking stop," she whispered as she guided his hand to her lace and satin covered mound. Desire darkened her eyes to the color of a stormy sea and she arched into his touch. "EJ, I want you."

His thoughts scattered into the wind of the storm raging outside, and his heart pounded in time with the downpour pelting the tin roof. He flicked open the front clasp of her bra and bared her breasts to him. As he cupped the left one and rolled the puckered nipple between his thumb and finger, he kissed down her neck, across the rise of her right breast. When he took the dark pink nipple into his mouth and suckled, she moaned his name and arched her back under him.

While he worked her breasts with his fingers and mouth, he slipped his hand under her panties. Not expecting to feel bare skin, he pulled away. "Damn, you're smooth."

She ran her nails over his chest to his cock. As she stroked up and down the length of him, she gave him a seductive smile. "You are too."

At the fiery sensations, he clenched his teeth. "Fuck."

"I intend to." She used his distraction to push him onto his back. "I prefer playing cowgirl." As she kissed him, she removed her thong, then straddled him.

"You know what they say, to save a horse, you have to ride a cowboy." His voice came out in a raspy growl.

She nuzzled his neck and let out a throaty, sexy laugh.

As she teased the head of his cock by rubbing it over the soft, hot folds of her sex, he grabbed her hips and groaned. He'd never been with a woman who was completely bare before, and the erotic sensation had him fighting for control.

With another sexy-as-sin laugh, she leaned over him and nibbled on his ear. "You like?"

She was going to kill him. "God...yes. Emily..."

He squeezed her hips and gritted his teeth as she guided his cock into her slick heat.

She kissed him, sweeping her tongue in and out mimicking the same relentless rhythm in which they rocked together.

Shifting, he rolled her under him. As he leaned over her, he pulled her legs up over his shoulders. While he thrust into her fast and deep, she moaned and closed her eyes. Ecstasy slacked her mouth into a soft *o* with his name coming out in a throaty gasp. When her inner muscles clenched around him as she came, she gripped his shoulders until her nails bit into him.

Moving in and out of her time to his frantic heartbeat, he watched her bliss light up her beautiful face as she writhed in pleasure, then the need to orgasm became too much to fight. With a curse, he squeezed his eyes closed and emptied himself into her.

* * * *

Emily should tell EJ to leave. She shouldn't be enjoying cuddling up against him with her head on his chest listening to the steady beat of his heart while he drew lazy circles on her shoulder. Nor should she be thinking of asking him to spend the night in her bed, or of how right this all felt.

"I'm curious." He cleared his throat.

She shifted to look up into his face. "About what?"

He drew his brows together. "I've never been with a woman who shaved their..."

She laughed and kissed his nose. "Actually I wax. I've been doing it since I was about seventeen and started wearing skimpier stage costumes and dresses with the mesh cutouts that show a lot of skin. It's easier than worrying about a wardrobe malfunction. Adhesive panties don't stick to hair that well," she said, getting the reaction from him she'd expected.

"Adhesive panties?" He widened his eyes slightly while his mouth opened then closed again. "Okay, I've decided I don't want to know."

With a chuckle at his embarrassment, she kissed him. He wrapped his arm around her shoulders and held her to him while his other hand slid between them. She gasped when he slid his fingers between her folds to her clit.

He sucked on her lower lip. "I intend to thoroughly explore this new discovery."

"Emm…" She caught his lip between her teeth as he stroked her. The strong kick inside her belly startled her.

"Whoa." He moved his hand from its erotic pursuit and laid it over her belly where it lay against him. When the baby awarded him with another kick, he smiled. "How far along are you?"

She laid her hand over his. "Almost seven months. I'm due the first week of October."

He blinked and shifted her to lie on her back. "No wonder you can't hide the pregnancy anymore." The baby moved again under his gentle touch, and he laughed. "Do you know what you're having?"

"A girl." She swallowed at the stab of regret, while watching his face light up with wonder when the baby shifted again. "I've known for a long time. I had an amniocentesis early in my pregnancy to make sure she would be healthy."

"I never felt Austin move inside Raquel."

His quiet, husky words surprised her. "I don't understand."

EJ shifted to look at her and caressed his fingers over her face. "Raquel and I married a month after she discovered she was pregnant." He rolled over onto his back and looked up at the ceiling. She turned to her side and propped herself up on her elbow, but he wouldn't meet her gaze. "When I came home from my last deployment, Raquel was six months pregnant. She wouldn't let me sleep with her, saying she was too uncomfortable." He swallowed and closed his eyes. "I preferred sleeping in the living room anyway because I had horrible nightmares."

When he finally met her gaze, his eyes were filled with sorrow. "Raquel hated being pregnant, but I didn't make things easy on her either. I was a mess. Blamed myself for the mission's failure and couldn't talk about it. I still can't say anything about what happened in Jerusalem because it's top secret. Hell, the reason I can tell you this much is because those two diplomats were killed, and that made the news."

She rested her head on his chest and snuggled up against him, holding him and giving him strength.

He wrapped his arm around her and trembled. "I think Raquel took my refusal to tell her what was going on in my head as meaning I didn't care about her. She gained a lot of weight while she was pregnant and never connected with our baby, blaming him and me for ruining her life." As he spoke, his voice took on a resentful edge. "She refused to hold Austin after he was born. I took care of him from the day we brought him home. The doctors said she had postpartum depression, but she was depressed long before she had him. She hated her life and us."

Emily didn't want his pain and anger to ruin their night, but she wanted to know what happened. Maybe she could help him understand why Raquel did what she did. "I know she overdosed on pills."

He took a deep breath and let it out slowly. "She was addicted to Adderall and Zoloft. The doctor prescribed her the depression medicine, but the Adderall she got on the black market. Normally, they work well for those who need them when taken in the right dosages, but she…"

When his voice faded away, she completed his sentence. "She didn't take as prescribed and they made a deadly combination."

"I wish I would have known what she was doing." His voice rumbled low in his chest. "If I hadn't been absorbed in my own demons, I might have been able to save her life." He sat up and ran both hands through his hair, then stood and faced the storm raging outside the window. Lightning flashed and illuminated him for a few heartbeats, making him appear like one of the ghosts that haunted him. "Our marriage probably wouldn't have survived, but she--she wouldn't be dead."

As she sat in the middle of the bed, she stared at his broad shoulders and the way his back tapered to a perfect ass. She took a deep breath and tried not to think about how much she wanted him or the tingle of unwanted hope his admission about his marriage sent through her. He was hurting, and she wanted to alleviate his guilt. "EJ, I'm sorry. But if she was an addict there wasn't much you could do until she wanted help."

He glanced over his shoulder at her, and she slipped off the bed to stand beside him. When his gaze slid over her naked body, heat replaced the sadness for a moment in his eyes, but he looked back out the window, and his jaw ticked as if he was gritting his teeth.

Was he upset that he was attracted to her? Or was it something else? Did he think she was like his dead wife? She pushed the questions aside.

"When my manager admitted me to Fernwood in February, I had no intention of staying. I honestly believed I wasn't an addict. Even though I finally admitted it to the medical director when he told me I was pregnant, I didn't totally believe I was one." When he glanced at her again, she swallowed down her sudden wish for clothes. Baring her soul to him seemed more intimidating while doing it stark naked. "But I changed my thinking when I went into withdrawal. I never reached that point before because I would check myself out before the shakes and night sweats got too bad."

"What was different this time?" His voice echoed with the thunder out on the prairie. "Why did you stay?"

"I remembered how my dad's mom died."

With a furrowed brow, he faced her. "She was a local singer who overdosed on sleeping pills, right?"

Emily nodded and crossed her arms in front of her and shivered more from her discomfort of confessing her soul in the buff than from the cool air coming from the vent by her feet.

He turned toward the bed and pulled back the covers. "C'mon, let's get back into bed."

After she followed him between the crisp white sheets, he pulled her to him. She snuggled against his chest and relished his warmth seeping into her. "My grandmother lived a troubled life and eventually ended it when Dad was four years old. He told me for most of his life he thought his parents hated him: his mother because she blamed him for trapping her in a loveless marriage that cheated her out of becoming famous, and his father because he disliked Dad's dream of becoming a singer. My grandfather repeatedly berated Dad, telling him he'd end up like his mother--an addict and dead if he pursued his dreams." She closed her eyes against the sudden burn in her sinuses. "Instead it was me who followed in my grandmother's footsteps. If I didn't stop the drugs, they would've killed me."

Swallowing the knot in her throat, she rested her hand over her belly. "My baby would be all alone, if she even survived, and I couldn't do that to her. She'd grow up thinking I hated her and Fabian didn't want her. That was when I admitted I was an addict and made a conscious decision to get clean. My baby deserves a momma who loves her. And I do. More than anything."

"That's what fascinates me about you, Emily." He laid his hand over hers and her baby. "You are the most unselfish person I know."

She shivered and a tear escaped as he kissed her.

He couldn't be more wrong.

Chapter 13

Emily awoke to EJ spooning her from behind and his hand resting on her belly. His deep and slow breaths tickled her shoulder and neck. The enticing bulge of his impressive cock pressed into her behind. A sense of contentment like she'd never experienced settled over her as she listened to his breathing and watched the dust motes glittering like tiny snowflakes in the early morning sunbeams.

She could wake up every morning like this. God, she wanted to. She wanted him. Not only sexually, not only as her best friend, but also as the man she would share the rest of her life with. Closing her eyes, she fought the sorrow rushing into the places of her heart where a moment ago she'd had peace and love.

God help her, but she'd fallen in love with him. Damn it, what had she ever done to piss off the cosmos? Why would fate finally bring her a good and honest man, the kind of man she would want as the father of her child when she couldn't have him?

She sucked in a breath when EJ slowly moved his hand from her belly to cover her left breast. Her sensitive nipples instantly responded to his touch, and she moaned. She looked over her shoulder at him and her breath caught at the cowboy god in her bed. Mussed dark blond hair hung over his forehead and caramel colored stubble covered his face, while desire deepened the gray of his heavy lidded eyes. With a gorgeous smile, he kissed her shoulder. "Good morning, beautiful."

Heat filled her and settled in her core at his gruff words. Holy hell, could the man be any more perfect? "Ditto."

His deep chuckle vibrated through her. He turned her onto her back and kissed her. She nipped at his lower lip, then opened her mouth under his, and he plunged his tongue in, turning the passion up to toe-curling. After breaking the kiss, he moved his hot, wet lips to her breast. While pinching the hard nipple of her left breast between his thumb and finger, he sucked on the other one. As she moaned and arched her back into the tingling pleasure, she threaded her fingers into his silky hair and held him to her.

He moved his lips to the valley between her breasts and placed soft kisses, his stubble creating its own set of tingling sensations. "Your breasts are perfect."

She met his heavy gaze and feathered her fingers over his temple to his hair. "You're perfect."

With a grin, he took the other nipple into his mouth and sucked while he moved his hand over her belly to her mound. She spread her legs to allow his fingers access to the achy, wet folds of her sex. She gasped at the fiery vibrations caused by the combination of his sucking her nipple and his circling caress of her clit.

Too soon he moved and she opened her eyes as he settled between her legs. He lifted her leg and kissed the inside of her knee. "Before I'm done, you will be begging me."

"Promises, promises." She laughed low and breathy.

He smirked before kissing the sensitive skin of her inner thigh. "I never make a promise I don't keep." Another nipping kiss, this time closer to the apex of her legs. "And I'll guarantee before I'm done with you, you'll be screaming my name."

Her breathing quickened at his sexy crude words. Damn, she was already close and he hadn't even touched her yet. "You're quite sure of yourself."

EJ kissed the inside of her other leg before looking up at her. "Yes, ma'am, I am."

When he bent his head, she trembled with anticipation.

"I love this smooth pussy." He kissed her folds, before spreading them to suck her bud of nerves.

She cried out and clawed at the sheets. "EJ… Oh… I'm going to come."

Before the waves of pleasure built to the pinnacle, he stopped his ministrations and nipped her inner thigh. She whimpered a protest and writhed as he left her hanging for a moment, then he found her clit again, this time nipping and licking until she went even higher than before. He repeated the torturous process again of stopping before she tipped over the top.

"EJ!" She arched her back off the bed and twisted her hands into the bedding. "Please…"

"Please--what?" he said inches away from the center. His deep voice rumbled through her. "Tell me." He blew on her hot flesh, and she shivered at the first hints of orgasm, but the stimulation was not quite enough to send her off.

"Damn... you... You know... what." Her words came out breathless and pleading. "Let me... come."

He chuckled and then sucked her into his hot mouth at the same time as he slipped two fingers into her. She flew apart in a blinding wave of light and pleasure that had her thrashing and crying his name.

When she finally came back together and opened her eyes, EJ looked down at her with a sexy, cocky grin. She'd give him credit where due. "Wow."

He sucked her earlobe, causing her to shiver, which set off a flurry of orgasmic aftershocks. "I'm not done." He nipped her ear and tilted her hips. Another shudder went through her as the head of his cock touched her. "You ready for more?"

Although her arms felt like jelly, she wrapped them around his neck and used her nails to claw at his back, causing him to tremble. "Are you?"

As he kissed her, he thrust forward and entered her. She groaned and sucked on his tongue. He set a fast pace and before she thought physically possible, he had her flying again. She met him thrust for thrust as she clawed at his back. He tossed his head back and gritted his teeth as if fighting for control. With a groan, he leaned forward and buried his head into her neck. "Come with me."

"EJ... Oh, God..." The sensations built to blinding intensity higher than before, and she hung on as every nerve seemed to explode at once. Screaming his name, over and over she became vaguely aware of EJ letting out a long, feral growl, which might have been her name, as he shoved into her and stilled.

Gasping for air, he fell to the bed next to her. "Damn... That was amazing."

She turned her head to look at him and smiled. "Next time--" she said between heavy breaths--"you'll be begging me."

* * * *

After showering together and getting dressed, they headed down to the kitchen. EJ went out to feed his horses, while Emily checked in with her people in Nashville. She'd called both her manager and assistant last night to tell them about Mike's sighting outside Nashville and to instruct them to release her whereabouts to the media.

When he reentered the kitchen, he made a cup of coffee. Emily laid her cell phone on the counter by the refrigerator.

"I couldn't get hold of Kelly, but Trish said she got word out to TMZ last night and they will run the story today. Also she said someone from *Good Morning America* contacted her this morning requesting a statement about Mike after his spotting in Nashville made the news. She was putting them off, but I told her to go ahead and contact the producer. I won't do an interview, but I will issue a statement."

Every time he thought of Emily making herself bait for Mike, his stomach turned to cement. "I still wish you wouldn't do this."

She frowned and opened the fridge door. "We've already been over this. It's the only way to catch him."

Emily held the door open and rubbed a hand over her swollen abdomen. Dressed in stretchy black shorts, a purple tank top, and nothing else, she looked like she belonged in his kitchen and as hot as hell. When she rubbed her bare foot against the back of her other leg as if she had an itch, he fought the urge of grabbing her and having a repeat of their earlier escapades on the kitchen table.

She glanced his way, raised a coppery brow over heated jade eyes, and blew him a kiss. He chuckled and retrieved his cup of coffee from the Keurig. If he didn't do something to distract himself, she wouldn't have to even touch him to have him begging her for a repeat of their round of sex that morning. The memory made him hard.

She grabbed the jug of milk, a package of cheese, and a carton of eggs. After she set the items on the counter beside him, she peered into the fridge again and frowned.

"What are you looking for?" He grinned at the pucker she twisted her extremely kissable lips into.

She moved a few items around on a shelf. "Some peppers or hot sauce." Closing the door, she signed. "You wouldn't happen to have any, would you?"

He opened a cupboard door and took down a mason jar of sliced peppers. "Clare canned these earlier this summer. Jalapenos and chilies. But I'll warn you--they're hot enough to set your tongue on fire."

With a wide smile, she took the jar and looked at it. "These are perfect. The hotter, the better."

Glancing at her collection of items, he picked up the milk and poured some into his coffee. "What are you going to make?"

"An omelet. I'm starving, and for the past few weeks I've been craving hot peppers and eggs. This is perfect." She looked around before turning her gaze on him. "Where are your pans?"

He pointed to the cabinet next to the stove. "You should be able to find whatever you need in there."

"Would you like one?" She got out a skillet and set it on the burner.

"Sure. I'd love one." While she went about mixing up omelets, he made her a cup of tea. The sight of her being at home in his kitchen stabbed his heart with longing. He'd fallen in love with her and wanted her to stay in his life forever. How could he get through to her that she didn't have to base her baby's upbringing on her own? He'd love to be a father to her child, but he didn't expect her to keep her ex a secret or to keep him away from his daughter. After all, he wouldn't keep Raquel's memories from Austin, though he hoped Emily filled the void of mother in his little boy's life.

His son had taken a real liking to Emily, and she was great with him. Would she think the same way concerning Austin's relationship with her if she wasn't pregnant, or if he was divorced rather than widowed?

Because it was too soon to confront her, he pushed the thought to the back of his mind. He had no idea how she felt about him, but they definitely had a connection going way beyond friendship with benefits. Before he and Raquel married, he'd played the field enough to know how casual sex felt, and comparing those experiences with what he and Emily had was like equating water with fine Tennessee whiskey.

Emily plated the two concoctions, while he set his coffee and her tea on the table. When she put the dishes down, he grinned. "These smell and look delicious."

"Thanks. I'm not much of a cook, but I can make omelets." She sat down across from him and started eating. After a few bites, she fixed her tea with sugar and took a sip. They ate in relative silence until her phone started buzzing. She retrieved it from the counter and answered it. "Hey, Trish, what's going on?"

After a moment, she fell against the counter and her face went as white as the fridge door. He rushed to her and grabbed her before she slipped to the floor. After taking the phone from her shaking hand, he held it to his ear. "Who is this? I'm Sheriff EJ Cowley."

"I'm Emily's manager, Trish Russell." The woman on the other end sobbed. "Is Emily okay?"

He wrapped his arm around Emily to keep her standing. "She's in shock. What the hell did you tell her?"

The woman sniffled. "Oh, God, I shouldn't have called, but I needed to warn Emily. I called about Kelly Piper--Emily's assistant." She cleared her throat. "Kelly's boyfriend found her body about an hour ago at his townhouse. He's a musician and just got home from touring. She was going to hide out there. But--but Emily's stepfather found her."

Trish gasped and was obviously having a hard time fighting her grief. "He's a madman."

"How do you know the murderer is Mike Ritter?" He helped get Emily back to her chair. Her pale face took a sickly gray shade and her breaths were more like pants as she curled around her middle and hugged her abdomen. He caressed her ashen cheek. Could this kind of shock harm the child? An icicle of fear stabbed his gut at the possibility.

"He left a message pinned to Kelly's body with the knife he used to-- oh, God--to slit her throat." Trish sobbed again and her voice cracked. "In it he said he was coming for Emily and she would be next."

Bile boiled in his gut making the breakfast he'd eaten churn unpleasantly at the thought of Emily's friend dying such a horrible death for nothing more than a psychopath's delivery of a message. "Are you in a safe place?"

Trish sniffled. "Yes, my family and I are leaving for Louisiana. My parents own a cabin on the bayou. Is Emily safe?"

"Yes, she's with me." He stared into Emily's terrified eyes, then made a vow to the stranger on the phone and to himself. "I'll keep her safe."

God help him. He would move heaven and earth to make sure nothing happened to her.

Chapter 14

Emily stared up at EJ and shivered as if the temperature in the room had dropped fifty degrees. Her limbs tingled with numbing fear.

Mike had killed Kelly simply to get to her.

EJ laid her phone on the table and wrapped Emily up into a hug. She forced her arms to encircle him and buried her face into his neck. He pulled Emily to her feet, then picked her up to carry her into the living room, where he sat on the couch with her across his lap.

"Emily? Sweetheart, are you okay?" His gentle words spoken near her ear sent another violent shiver through her.

Unable to hold back the sobs any more, she cried. "Why did he have to kill her?"

"I don't know." He held her closer and caressed her back. "He won't hurt you. I won't let him."

With her face pressed into the front of his shirt, she breathed in his fresh scent and clung to him. "Is Trish safe? God, I didn't even ask."

"Yes, she's heading to the Louisiana bayou."

Swallowing the lump in her throat, she nodded against his chest. "This is all my fault."

He tilted her chin up with his thumb to force her to meet his stern gaze. "No. This is not your fault. Mike Ritter is a sick, sick man, Emily. You have nothing to do with his rampage."

She shook her head. How could he not see? "If I hadn't forced Kelly to keep my whereabouts secret, Mike wouldn't have gone to Nashville." She moved off his lap and paced the length of living room. "If I hadn't been selfish." Like the last time, but this time someone died.

Standing, EJ stopped her as she passed the couch and pulled her into his arms. As he caressed her hair, he held her head to his shoulder. "You are not selfish. You were doing what was best for your family. I wish your being here was still a secret."

She tried to pull out of his embrace, but he held on, and she sobbed at his words. He had no idea. "Yes. I am selfish." As the memories flooded her, she shuddered. God, she'd do anything for either a drink or a line of coke right now. She fought the craving by focusing on him and taking comfort from him. "Like the last time. All I thought about was myself."

"I don't believe that." He stroked her hair and held her tight.

His husky words seeped through her, making her want to confess. He had to know she wasn't what he thought she was. She sniffed and wiped the back of her hand over her nose. "You're wrong. When Mike shot my dad eight years ago, all I could think about, as Mom and I sat in the hospital waiting to hear if he would live or die, was that he couldn't die because he'd promised to make my dreams come true." She had to make him see she didn't deserve his kindness. As she stepped out of his embrace, she shook her head and sobbed. "I didn't care that he was my dad. The only thing I worried about was, if he died, I would never get famous."

Hugging her middle, she bent over as the sobs came uncontrollably. She'd never told anyone her darkest secret. Not even the shrinks she'd had over the years. EJ was different. She loved him and had to protect him from the poison inside her.

"God, Emily." He reached for her, but she shook her head and backed away from him.

"No, don't you see?" She met the compassionate pewter eyes, she'd come to rely on. "My fame--my life--is built on greed. Is it any wonder I've ruined it? It's Karma."

EJ stepped toward her and shook his head. "No! Emily. No. You were a kid."

"I was fourteen! I was old enough to know I was wrong."

He grabbed her arms and held her. "I don't care if you were thirty. Your parents dropped a bomb on you. Then Seth announced you were his daughter on stage in front of ten thousand people, many of them your friends and family. Dear God, what was the man thinking?" EJ pulled her to him and wrapped her up in his arms. She didn't fight him as he kissed her temple. "On top of it all, Mike tried to kidnap you and shot Seth. Emily, you were in shock." He pulled away far enough to look into her eyes. "Do you know what I thought about before things went south in Jerusalem?"

She shook her head since words were impossible. How could this man still believe in her?

"I was pissed at Raquel because she'd sent me the wrong damned book. I wanted the latest novel from whoever I was reading at the time, but she'd sent me one I'd already read." He took a deep breath and shifted his eyes from hers. "When we were ambushed and the shooting started, I wasn't thinking of my unborn child or my family. I could have been killed and my last thoughts would have been absorbed with a petty anger." He swallowed hard and met her gaze again. As he used his thumb to wipe her tears away, he said, "My point is we are all human, Emily. You are no different. We all think or say things we later regret, but the truth is that in those singular traumatic moments when our brains stop thinking rationally, we get stuck on things we would never even consider at other times. All of us have said things in the heat of anger we would never say at saner times. The same is true when life pulls the rug out from under us. You did not mean what you were thinking when your dad was shot anymore than I did the curses I through at Raquel over the book.

"I don't consider your thoughts deranged or even selfish." He kissed her temple, his lips as soft and gentle as butterfly wings. "You were hanging onto something you desperately wanted, because at that moment, when your life was turned inside out, it was the only thing that made sense." He kissed her again and held her tight as his breath warmed her temple. "I wish you could see what I do when I look at you. I tried to stay away from you. I tried to convince myself you were like Raquel." He feathered his fingers over her tear-soaked cheeks as he met her gaze. The intensity in his eyes caused her heart to skip a few beats. No man had ever looked at her like this. "You are nothing like her. Despite your struggles, you love your baby enough to want to get and stay drug free. You are willingly putting yourself in danger to ensure your family stays safe. Dear God, Emily, you are the strongest, most honest person I know."

His husky words pounded on the thick wall of self-doubt and shame she'd built around her heart. She didn't deserve this man, but she didn't know how she could get through this without him.

"I'm strong because you're here. I draw from you. You make me want to do better." She clung to him, wanting him, loving him. What would she do when she left him?

* * * *

EJ tossed his cell phone on his desk in his house office and stared out the window at the pasture beyond the back yard. Emily had finally gone to sleep, and he spent the past three hours making phone calls. First, he contacted the Nashville police and the FBI to get a report on Kelly Piper's murder. Afterward, he spoke to a tense Seth and Abby Kendall, ensuring them Emily was safe, and although she took the news of her assistant's death hard, she was resting. They would call Emily later.

The last call was to his lieutenant deputies Clint Grier and Bucky McCoy. They needed to meet and come up with a plan. As he watched the sun and summer breeze play in the buffalo grass of the pasture, one of Emily's security guards crossed the yard. EJ hadn't spoken to the two men much before showing them to the bunkhouse. They'd rented a car at the airport and driven to his ranch, and when they showed up, EJ was too surprised with the memory of them denying him access to Emily at her concert to say much.

EJ went into the kitchen and opened the back door. "Hey."

Emily had told him Oliver Devore and Jason Harmon were her most trustworthy guards. Hired by her father when he still oversaw her career five years ago, both men were in their forties, and as she'd put it, treated her more like a kid sister or a daughter than their boss.

Oliver Devore headed his way with the bearing of an ex-military man. When he reached the porch, he stood at what was definitely a military stance and nodded a greeting. "Sheriff?"

EJ studied the big bald man. With the coffee-mocha complexion of someone of mixed races, he matched EJ's six-two, but out-muscled him. He stared back at EJ with deep-set dark brown eyes, and a stoic expression caused the lines on either side of his wide mouth to furrow. EJ suspected the man's age to be closer to fifty than forty. "What branch did you serve in?"

Oliver lifted a dark brow. "Navy SEALs, I retired as a commander. You were in the Army Rangers, right?"

With a grin, EJ held out his hand and Oliver shook it. "Yeah. I got out two years ago at the rank of captain."

Oliver chuckled, a deep rumbling sound. "You and Jason should talk," he said referring to Jason Harmon, Emily's other bodyguard. Jason had taken the first round of watching the house last night and probably was sleeping. "He's an Army guy." Before EJ had a chance to comment, Oliver sobered and returned to his military stance with is hands at his sides. "I heard about Kelly. Do you know anything about Ritter?"

EJ cleared his throat. "That's why I called for you. I'm meeting with my deputies in a few minutes and wanted to include you."

"I'll be there." He shifted his feet and glanced toward the house. "How is she?"

With a deep breath, EJ opened the screen door. "Grieving. She's taking this hard."

Oliver nodded and glanced out over the yard. "Emily doesn't have many friends she can trust. Kelly was one of those few friends."

EJ had suspected as much. "Come in." Once they were inside, EJ took two mugs from the cabinet. "Coffee?"

Oliver stood in the center of the kitchen and nodded. "That would be great." As EJ brewed the first cup of coffee, the other man looked around. "Nice place. I couldn't help notice the name on the gate. The Arrowhead. I thought ranches were always called things like Double K or Circle something or other." EJ sensed Oliver watching him. "Has this place been in your family for long? I know Emily's ranch has been her family forever."

EJ removed the full mug from the machine and held it out to Oliver. "I bought the Arrowhead from my aunt and uncle. It's been in my mother's family for six generations. The Campbells settled this land about the same time the Kendalls did the Double K." EJ got the milk from the fridge and held it out to Oliver, who shook his head. After pouring some into his coffee, EJ put it back. "My great-great-great grandfather called it the Arrowhead because he found an old Indian campsite on the land. I still find arrowheads and broken pieces of pottery in the spot."

"Cool." Oliver sipped his coffee. EJ indicated a chair and they sat. With a broad smile, Oliver shook his head. "I was an Army brat and lived all over. When my dad retired, my parents settled in Georgia, but I was already in the Navy." The SEAL set his cup on the table and narrowed his eyes on EJ. "What's going on between you and Emily?"

He didn't want to answer the man's question, but as they stared at each other, EJ got the impression Oliver could be an ally if he wanted him to be one. He didn't know Oliver's background, but he did know a few things about him. One, he was hired by Emily's father, who's judgment EJ trusted. Two, he was a SEAL, and three, he was loyal to Emily even when her ex fired him.

EJ met the man's unwavering gaze. "I want to have a future together."

Oliver smiled and sat back in his chair. "I'm glad. She needs someone like you."

EJ snorted and picked up his mug to take a sip. "Like me? What the hell is that supposed to mean?"

With a shrug, Oliver drained his cup. "I've done some research on you, Cowley." His teeth flashed white in his tanned face when he grinned. "You have an impressive military record. Of course, like a lot of us in Special Ops, most of it is sealed. I do know you led the mission back in twenty-seventeen to rescue the American ambassador to Israel and her assistant when Islamic extremists kidnapped them from the embassy in Jerusalem."

EJ stood and headed for the coffee maker. He needed another cup of coffee. "Then you know how it all went to hell."

"Yes. But I also know out of fifteen missions, it was the only one that did. Why did you get out? From what I read you were soon up for promotion."

EJ didn't like being at the disadvantage with the bodyguard. Oliver knew too much about him, and EJ didn't know a damned thing about the ex-SEAL. EJ turned to glare at him. "I got out for personal reasons."

"Your wife was pregnant." Oliver folded his arms over his wide chest. "She committed suicide and left you with an infant son."

"I think you know more than you should."

Oliver shrugged and held his hands out. "I think you are good for Emily because you understand her. You've overcome tragedy, and you can help her to do the same. Emily is like a daughter to me. I want to protect her. She's a strong woman, but her heart is fragile."

EJ took a deep breath and dialed back his annoyance at the bodyguard. He'd probably be as protective if he was in this man's shoes. Emily's daughter instantly came to mind. He already had an incredible connection with the unborn baby. What would he be like with her daughter in twenty years? Would Emily give him a chance to be her baby's surrogate father?

"Emily is my first and only priority."

Oliver nodded once, stood, and held out a big hand, with a wide, open smile spreading over his face. "Then you and I will get along fine."

* * * *

Emily awoke from a dream with a start. Sitting up in the strange king-sized bed, she looked around the darkened room. Vertical blinds covered the bay windows. Beside the big screen TV, the door to the hall stood slightly ajar. The wall opposite the windows held two more doors and large dresser.

EJ's room. He'd brought her here instead of taking her to her own bed after she had the breakdown in the kitchen. She blew out a long breath and lay back on the pillow. Why did she confess her soul to him? Of course, he'd try to make her feel better by telling her she wasn't deeply flawed for being selfish.

She turned over onto her side and hugged the pillow next to her. Burying her nose into the white cotton of the pillowcase, she filled her lungs with EJ's scent of the outdoors. She didn't deserve a man like EJ. He had a way of making her forget who and what she was. Around him, she could *feel* normal.

But she wasn't normal. Never was, and she couldn't forget it.

Unable to stay in his bed any longer, she got up. She looked around the room again, and headed for the door EJ had told her was the en suite bathroom, which at one time had undoubtedly been an adjoining bedroom. After she finished, she headed down the stairs to the kitchen to find something to eat.

From the direction of the office off the kitchen, she heard Clint Grier's baritone voice. "The national news networks are running stories about Kelly Piper's death." Wanting to know more, she ignored her rumbling belly and stood next the open door of EJ's office. "They're reporting that Emily is hiding out in McAllister. It's only a matter of time before Ritter knows where to find her."

"I know," EJ said. A chair squeaked and EJ's familiar footsteps followed as if he was pacing. Closing her eyes, she leaned against the wall. The sound of EJ's boots tapping across the hard wood was oddly comforting and disconcerting at the same time. "Emily won't leave. She believes she has to be the one to draw him out."

"That's freakin' crazy," said a man she didn't know in a strong Texas drawl she placed well south of McAllister. She assumed he was one of EJ's other deputies. "EJ, wouldn't it be better if she left town? Hell, she was here for almost a month without anybody knowing. If she left town now without telling anyone, everyone would think she was still here, as would Ritter. We could be ready for him when he comes hunting for her."

For a moment, she considered the suggestion. Maybe she should leave, but she knew she wouldn't.

"Emily won't do that," said Oliver. She was glad EJ included her bodyguards in the meeting. They knew her better than anyone, even EJ. "She won't run from something she feels strongly about."

"Devore's right." EJ stopped pacing right inside the door. She pressed against the wall and held her breath. "The time for her to escape is past. Y'all saw the news trucks parked outside the gates of the Double K and the Circle R," EJ said referring to the ranch belonging to Mike's parents. "Even if she tries a disguise there's no guarantee she wouldn't be recognized." He paced away from the door, and a moment later a chair scrapped the floor. "If she did get away, who do you think Ritter would go after next to draw her out?"

"His parents." Clint Grier's voice held a touch of defeat.

Despite everything Mike had done, she considered Frank and Carolann Ritter her grandparents, and he knew it. She wished they would leave town, but Frank's health had quickly deteriorated in the past years. His Parkinson's disease debilitated him to the point he could barely feed himself.

"Do you think he'd hurt his parents?" The unknown voice sounded surprised. He must not know Mike as well as she did. She wouldn't put anything past him.

"Yes. Bucky. You're new to McAllister, but you have to know the story. Mike Ritter is one sadistic son of a bitch." Clint cleared his throat. "I worked with him for ten years. First, as a fellow deputy, and then as his lieutenant. I never had an inkling about his organized crime connections. Not once did I sense he didn't love his daughter. I had my suspicions about his marriage to Abby. Something had always been off there, but the rest... No. I've known Mike Ritter all of my life and never knew how he'd manipulated people. Even me. My point is simple. Mike will do anything to get what he wants--which is Emily."

"I don't believe Emily knows why Seth Kendall hired Jason and me." Emily had to strain to hear Oliver's low voice. "Kelly screened all of Emily's fan mail." Emily closed her eyes against the ache in her chest hearing her friend's name caused. "Every artist gets hate mail. Some of it is even threatening. The letter Kelly brought to Seth from Ritter wasn't overly threatening, but it didn't have a good vibe. In it, he mentioned he knew exactly where Emily was and that someday he'd find her. What convinced Seth to hire two bodyguards for her was the inclusion of photographs."

Oliver paused, and Emily couldn't breathe as she fought the panic threatening to overtake her. She hadn't known any of this.

"Somehow Ritter got personal photos of her. One was of her shopping with Kelly. The other was of her undressing in her dressing room after a show. She was sixteen."

The other men spoke, but she couldn't concentrate on what they said. *Oh, God!* She grabbed at her chest as terror turned her blood to ice and made her knees shake. Running and hiding would be easy. Safe. She had no doubt Mike would kill her if he got his hands on her. Her only hope was in EJ catching him before Mike could carry out the action.

EJ was right. She wasn't going anywhere. She'd been running and hiding all her life. Her addiction and her marriage to a man she'd had nothing in common with had been a form of hiding from her past.

With a deep breath to bolster her resolve, she glanced down at the open shirt she'd put on over her tank top. She might be done hiding, but she didn't think EJ's men or her bodyguards knowing about her pregnancy would help her case any. Getting her idea past EJ was going to be hard enough. Satisfied her baby bump was sufficiently camouflaged, she stepped into the office.

The group of men turned to look at her, and EJ stood from his chair behind the desk he usually used to manage his ranch, not to run the sheriff's department. "Emily…"

"I want to do a news conference." She fisted her hands to keep them from shaking. "Mike Ritter needs to know exactly where to find me. No one else will die because of me."

Please, God, she prayed as she stared at the group of frowning men, *keep my baby safe.*

Chapter 15

The other men couldn't leave fast enough for EJ. He needed to get Emily alone. Although he wanted to wring her neck, he'd settle with verbally pounding some sense into her. Either way he didn't want an audience. EJ paced the length of the kitchen, then turned and paced back. His hands clenched and unclenched in time with his jaw. If he had high blood pressure, he would have had a stroke by now. Counting to ten for at least the tenth time hadn't done anything to curb his anger.

He whirled and narrowed his eyes on the woman he loved. "Are you fucking out of your mind?"

She shifted in her seat at the kitchen table and folded her arms in front of her. "No. EJ, I know you don't agree with me, but you have to admit it's the only way to flush Mike out. He could show up around here and stay hidden for days, maybe weeks. In the mean time, if he can't figure out where I am, he could hurt someone I care about." She stood and strode toward him. "I couldn't live with that."

He let out a breath between clenched teeth. "What if he hurts you?" Laying his hand on her baby bump, he met her gaze; something deeper replaced the anger in his gray eyes. "Are you willing to risk your baby?"

His husky voice caused a cold shudder to tingle down her back. "You won't let it come to that."

With a guttural sound, he spun away from her and raked both hands into his hair. "Damn it, Emily! I wish you didn't have such faith in my ability to keep you safe."

She needed to know why she couldn't trust him. Damn the secrecy of his mission to hell. He had to tell her what happened in Jerusalem. He turned and took her into his arms. She shook from the stress of the day. As he placed a soft kiss on her temple, he breathed in her beautiful scent. "What I'm about to tell can't leave this room. Understand?"

She nodded against his shoulder.

"The mission in Jerusalem failed because I hadn't anticipated every possible contingency. Complacency made me sloppy. I led my team into the tunnels under the city where the terrorists were hiding the ambassador and her assistant without fully memorizing the layout of the exit points. I thought I knew them, but hadn't prepared myself or my team enough on how to get out. To me, it was another grab and go mission. Like all the others I'd conducted. But this one was different from the beginning." All the things he should have done flooded him, and he had to stop speaking to clear the knot out of his throat.

She stepped out of his embrace, took his hand, and led him into the living room. He pulled her back into his arms and sat on the couch with her across his lap, needing her strength to recount a memory he hadn't told anyone.

With gentle fingers, she stroked his face. "You don't have to say more. I can tell this is causing you a lot of pain."

He forced a smile. "I've never talked to anyone about what happened, but you have to understand I don't know if I can protect you."

She kissed him softly. "And you have to understand I won't judge your ability on one failed mission out of several successful ones."

How could she not see? His self-doubt was enough to incapacitate him. "What if I don't take into account everything again? Emily, if I don't anticipate something before it happens, or worse, overthink something. It could mean your life."

As a shiver went through her, she rested her head on his shoulder. "No one can see everything. Not even you."

"Maybe not. But I was trained to anticipate the unexpected."

Telling her what happened went against his oath to keep the mission top secret and was doing little in convincing her she shouldn't have faith in him. Nothing would ever purge the pain and guilt he'd held inside since the mission, but finally speaking about the events that destroyed his faith in himself liberated him. As if by telling her, he was finally giving his team and the people he'd been sent to free a voice, making him feel whole again.

He swallowed hard, then plunged into the past. "We got in, took out the guards and found the captives." At the memory of the joy on the middle-aged face of American Ambassador Evelyn Davidson, he closed his eyes. "The ambassador was beaten and most likely raped, and her assistant was tortured." He shook his head. Emily didn't need the gory details of the captives' treatment at the hands of the terrorists and he had no desire to relive the barbaric conditions of the tunnels. "My team did its job by clearing out the underground, but I got turned around down there and didn't know our chosen escape route. I eventually found it, but it gave the terrorists enough time to get a call out to their topside contingent. When we came out, they were waiting for us. Within minutes five members of my team were dead, including the ambassador. Her assistant was wounded, but he died later that day in the hospital." He took a deep breath and closed his eyes as he thought of the ambassador and her battered assistant. "They saw me as their savior. Little did they know, I'd lead them to their deaths."

"You were their savior."

He opened his eyes to look into her honest and open expression. "How can you say that?"

A small smile played on the corners of her lips. "Even if I knew I was going to die, I wouldn't want to be a helpless captive. You freed them, EJ, and even though they were still killed at their kidnappers' hands, they died escaping."

With a snort, he ran his fingers through her silky hair, marveling at her innocent honesty. He kissed her and wanted to tell her how much he loved her, but like gentling a colt, he had to bide his time. Instead, he poured all of his feelings into the kiss. The ferociousness with which she returned his passion encouraged him. Did she love him as well, but was too stubborn to admit it? God, he hoped she did. He had his own tenacity. Being the youngest of five kids also taught him patience. Although the waiting was hard, he'd rather not have Mike Ritter's threat hanging over their heads when he declared his heart to her.

When she sucked in his lip, desire heated his insides as if he'd stepped too close to a fire. Pulling away, he held her face between his hands and fought to catch his breath. The blaze shining in her green eyes burned with the intensity of a prairie fire ready to consume him whole. "God, I want you."

Mischievousness danced in her gaze as she smiled. "I seem to remember you owe me some payback."

The low sexy voice did as much to him as a touch, and he shivered.

"I don't recall owing you anything." He knew exactly what she was talking about, and the prospect had him aching before she even got started.

She gave him a sassy grin and slid out of his arms. With agonizing slowness, she slipped the shirt off her shoulders and let it drop to the carpet. He took his cue and unbuttoned his own shirt. When she reached for the bottom of her tank top, he stood and kissed her. She put her hands on his chest and pushed. Not expecting the assault, he fell back onto the couch.

"Oh, no." She quirked a russet brow. "You are totally at my mercy, Sheriff Cowley. Do I need to find your handcuffs?" When he chuckled, she pulled the tank top off and straddled his lap. As he kissed her, he reached for her bare back, but she intercepted his hands and shoved them over his head. She distracted him by moving against him and sucking on his tongue, then used the stretchy cotton shirt to bind his hands above his head.

While he looked up at her handiwork, she slid off his lap. "That should keep your hands from roaming at least."

"Never thought you were into bondage." He brought his arms down to lay in front of him.

"You know what they say about the quiet types."

He let out a snort and tested the bond. The knot was surprisingly tight. "Well, since you aren't the quiet type, I suppose I shouldn't be at all surprised."

"Uh-uh." She pushed his hands behind his head. "You keep them behind you or"--she ran a finger down his bare chest, which caused him to suck in a breath, while her husky tone made his body burn for her as she spoke near his ear--"begging won't be enough."

She was absolutely beyond hot.

With a toss of her head, she turned and sashayed toward the stereo system.

"Turn it on." His voice was hoarse even to his ears.

When her soulful voice filled the room, she looked over her shoulder at him with widened eyes.

"Every time I listen to it, I want to bury myself into you."

When she turned with her mouth ajar, he chuckled. For a woman who had experienced more than most did in a hundred years and had more than a little sense of sexual adventure as his bound hands proved, she blushed as scarlet as her hair. "You like *My Summertime Lover?*"

He grinned at the incredibility in her voice. "It's my favorite song, I think. I can't believe the song was never recorded."

She turned toward the shelving. "I wanted to record it, but my record company thought the song too mature for my age. I added it to the CD because I wanted ten songs."

"When did you write it?" He'd assumed she'd written it while she was married, although the thought the sexy love song was for her ex sent a stab of steely jealousy through him. If she was a teenager when she penned the provocative tone…. He wasn't sure what that said about him because the song sure as hell turned him on.

With a curious half smile, she faced him. "Six years ago."

Holy shit, she was only sixteen then. Not about her ex. He doubted it was about the two Hollywood teenage boys she'd dated either. Who else could it be about? "Is it about Trevor?" He hadn't wanted to ask the question aloud, but once the words slipped out it was too late. With a shake of his head, he sniffed, not wanting to think about Emily and his prissy brother-in-law. Had he been completely wrong about Trevor's sexual orientation? "Never mind. I don't want to know."

She snorted. "No. The song's not about Trevor Marshall." With a sly smile, she walked toward him, placing each step before the other which gave her hips a seductive swing. She removed her lacy bra and pushed her shorts down her legs, stepping out of them before she reached him. All the while her disembodied voice and the angel dressed in lacy panties sang the chorus in perfect harmony:

Lay me down in the sweet green grass,
Kiss me, baby, love me all over,
Till I shatter like a pane of glass.
Forever be my summertime lover.

Breathless and painfully hard, he gasped, "Who?"

Stopping between his spread knees, she reached for his belt buckle. "Oh, that's my little secret." She opened the button of his jeans, never taking her gaze from his. Something in the intense celadon depths of her eyes had his heart skip a beat. "I will tell you the subject of the song was a fantasy of mine."

Before he could say anything else, she leaned over and gripped his zipper between her teeth. He couldn't breathe as she opened his jeans with delirious slowness. The sight of her had him on edge. Hell, if she kept this up, he wouldn't need to beg; he'd be coming with a mere touch from her.

When she took him into her hands, he laid his head back between his bound hands and closed his eyes. She kissed the head of his cock, causing a tingling anticipation in every nerve of his body, and he let out a loud moan. "God, Emily…"

She ran her lips, barely touching down the sensitive ridge. "I've only just begun, cowboy. You'll be begging before long."

After she teased and sucked him until he thought he'd burst, he did beg, but she still didn't relent. He pulled his hands out of his insubstantial bounds and grabbed her head on either side.

She lifted her lips from his cock and grinned. "You were to stay put."

"Yeah, well." His voice rasped. "I'm done begging and have decided it's time to take what I want."

Her laugh was low and husky as she stood and removed her panties. She straddled his thighs, leaned over him and combed her fingers into his hair. "I'm glad, because I don't know how much longer I could've held out."

As she lowered herself onto his cock, he groaned at the hot, slick heaven. Taking him deep into her, she kissed him. He gripped her ass and set a pounding pace. Less than a half dozen thrusts later, she tightened around him, and they both cried out.

Chapter 16

Three days later Emily sat behind the conference table in the sheriff's Department answering carefully scripted questions from *Famous in America* host, Becca Larkin. Trish arranged the interview with the ABC Network primetime show from her Louisiana hideout. The opportunity of interviewing Emily excited the network enough they agreed to air it the next night. Seemingly, nothing was sacred. She answered inquiries about her divorce, rehab, and coming home to Texas. Although the producer wanted to record the show at the Double K, she insisted the taping take place in the sheriff's offices and the content be supplied ahead of time. Also, Emily supplied a few suggestions herself, assuring the meeting go as she wanted it to.

"You've taken a break from entertainment. What's next for you?" Becca Larkin's smile was wide with bleached teeth showing and red-lipped.

Motherhood. If I live through Mike Ritter's revenge. Emily matched Becca's practiced grin, but inside she was a bundle of nerves. "I'm getting my life back." She glanced at EJ standing behind the camera man and the producer. He nodded with a smile, giving her courage to keep up the charade. "Yes, I'm taking a break. This is a tough business, and I've been in it for a long time."

"You have fans all over the world. Do you have anything in store for them to tide them over until you're back?"

She was too hot, being dressed in layers to prevent the prospect of the reporter or her entourage detecting Emily's ever expanding belly. EJ had convinced her to trust his sister-in-law Judy. He'd suggested Judy might be able to help her figure out ways to hide the pregnancy. Judy had hidden her first pregnancy up until the end from her parents and everyone else, too. Apparently, the Mackenzie's hadn't liked EJ's eldest brother much. In their minds, Tucker had limited prospects as husband material since he was only a ranch hand on the Double K, besides being seven years older than Judy with no ambition to settle down.

Despite the sweat gathering under her breasts and running down her back, Emily was glad she'd enlisted Judy for help. Together they ordered clothes online and had them overnight shipped. The older woman suggested Emily use a Spanx bodysuit to help hold her belly in as much as possible. Judy assured her wearing shapewear once in a while wouldn't harm the baby, which had been Emily's first concern; however, she couldn't wear the restricting thing for long. It was too damned uncomfortable. Next, Judy found a long gray pencil skirt, then a black flowing top, and multi-colored scarf accessorized the ensemble. The outfit was nothing she'd ever choose to wear. It made her look somewhat frumpy. Although she had to admit, because of the long line of the skirt, the pleating of the shirt, and the large scarf artfully looped around her neck with the ends trailing down, the curve of her belly was total lost in it all.

"We're all waiting for new music…"

The reporter's prompting brought Emily back to the present and she swallowed. "I'll be releasing an EP of my last six pop songs in September."

The reporter's dark eyes widened slightly. "Are you crossing back into the country genre?"

A healthy kick in the ribs nearly brought a wince to Emily's carefully poised expression. *We're almost done, baby girl. I know you're probably being squished.* Emily clenched her hand into a fist where it lay on her lap to keep from rubbing her belly to sooth the active baby. She caught the concerned frown and ready stance of EJ. He hadn't missed her moment of discomfort and would rescue her if she needed him to. Like a knight in shining armor. No, more like a cowboy. Her cowboy. A real smile replaced the painfully fake one. God, she loved him.

"I haven't decided yet." Which wasn't a total lie. She missed singing and couldn't imagine her life without it. But how could she raise her daughter and entertain as well? She didn't want to take the baby on the road, hoping to protect her daughter from the evils of fame for as long as possible. Instead, she thought of the record company. The deal was a few weeks from being finalized. Midland Records agreed to release Emily from her contract. They would sever ties with Gabe after his album release and her dad after his tour. They could possibly be fully in business by next summer. "I do have something in the works, but I'm not at liberty to say anything about it today."

Becca nodded appreciatively and changed tact. "On July third your stepfather escaped from a work detail outside Clements Prison in Amarillo.

We were shocked when he murdered your personal assistant Kelly Piper," she said, with her face and tone schooled in professional sympathy, then she paused as if to give a moment of silent honor or possibly for dramatic effect, Emily didn't know which. "What precautions are you taking?"

Emily crossed her legs under the table, burying her shaking hands between her thighs. "Sheriff Cowley has been providing protection. He's been most gracious in letting me live at his home while my parents are on tour." She glanced at EJ, who frowned. He wasn't happy with this plan of letting the world know where she was, but he did understand the necessity of it.

Mike was moving across the country like a ghost. Two days ago, he'd been spotted in Memphis at a gas station, but by the time the police arrived, he'd vanished again. Interstate 40 had check points at every entrance and at the state lines, but the FBI quickly ascertained he wasn't traveling the most direct route between Nashville and McAllister. The Arkansas and Missouri state police and FBI were setting up check points on the back roads, but the going was slow and required more manpower than available. He hadn't been seen since Memphis. Emily was resigned that Mike wouldn't be caught until he was in town and had her directly in his sights.

Ten minutes later, the taping was over. The broadcast was scheduled for tomorrow evening, but the text of the interview would be released on line by morning. EJ came to Emily as she said a hasty goodbye to Becca Larkin and her producer, then she hurried out of the station, and he helped her into his Silverado.

She stared out the windshield and shivered, hoping she'd done the right thing. EJ climbed into the big truck and squeezed her hand were it lay limp as a dishrag on her lap. "Christ, you're hands are like ice."

Turning to look at him, she swallowed the lump in her throat and shivered again. "Now that I've told the world where to find me, I'm scared shitless."

He picked up her hand and kissed her knuckles. "I'm not too happy about it either, but I'm here to protect you. I won't let anything happen to you."

She nodded and forced a smile. "That's the only thing keeping me sane."

* * * *

EJ drove her to Amarillo to the OB doctor she'd been referred to by her Nashville physician two days later. Although her mother had also seen Dr. Jane Holt, Emily was nervous about appointment. Most likely every staff member in the office would have seen the broadcast last night and would have noticed her exclusion of talking about her pregnancy. Not that the staff wouldn't keep her secret--after all they were bound by the HIPAA privacy law and a non-disclosure agreement Trish had sent the office personnel to sign--but for the first time, she was uncomfortable with her secrecy.

In the parking lot, EJ pulled his Silverado into the space closest to the service entrance of the three-story medical building. When he left the engine running as he peered out of the windshield, she got the impression he was looking for more than paparazzi with long range cameras.

He turned the ignition off and glanced at her. "You haven't been here before?"

She shook her head and folded her cold hands in her lap. "No. I should've had a checkup two weeks ago, but Dr. Holt couldn't get me in sooner than today." She reached for the door handle. "I better go. I might be a little while. The doctor wants to do a sonogram since I'm a new patient."

He looked out the window again. "I'm coming with you."

The prospect of him being with her during the exam thrilled her, but she didn't want him there if he did it out of some sort of protector obligation. "You don't have to do that. I think I'm safe here."

He faced her. "That's not why I want to go. I want to be there. I mean--" Rubbing his chin, he let his gaze slip from hers. "Raquel wouldn't let me go with her to the doctor when she was pregnant with Austin. Her mother went with her. Hell, I'm not sure either one of them wanted me in the delivery room with her when he was born." He shook his head as if getting rid of the bitterness, then let out a breath. Her heart sputtered over a beat when he looked at her again with eyes full of tenderness. "I know it's only been a couple of weeks, but I feel more connected to your baby than I did my own son at the same stage of his development." She opened her mouth to remind him they couldn't have more than friendship, despite their sexual escapades, but he held up a hand to stop her before she even got a word out. "Don't tell me we can't explore how far this--this thing between us can go. I know your reasons for holding back, and I don't agree with you."

He opened the door and got out, leaving her staring after him with her mind rolling at the meaning under his words. She startled when her door opened, and she turned to him. He held out his hand and gave her a devilish one-sided grin. "C'mon, I don't want you to be late. Besides, no one knows who the hell I am. Let the office staff speculate what I am to you."

She shifted her sunglasses farther up her nose and took his hand, letting him help her out of the truck. "What should I call you since your name was mentioned on the broadcast, Sheriff *EJ* Cowley?"she asked, stressing his nickname. With a grin, she stepped through the metal door he held open. A big black and white sign clearly marked it as an employee entrance. "Edward or Eddie?"

He stepped into the hallway with a scowl. "Neither. How about James or Jim. I can tolerate my middle name better than my first."

She laughed as they headed down the short hallway on the right to an elevator. He pushed the UP button, and she removed her glasses. "Why do you disliking your first name? Aren't you named for your grandfathers?"

Nodding in answer to her last question, he shrugged and looked a bit sheepish. "My eldest sister Becky gave me the nickname EJ when I was a baby and it stuck, but the reason for my profound dislike of Edward is a little more recent." He then looked at her and glared as if she had something to do with it. "Do you remember those vampire books and later movies--*Twilight*--I think was the title of one of them or maybe the whole series?"

"I loved that series of books as a kid. Every one of my girl friends either loved Jacob or…" Dawning came to her as the elevator pinged open and she laughed. "Oh, I get it." She batted her lashes at him. "*Edward*. He was my favorite," she said, perfecting a dreamy tone to irritate him further. "You know you actually look a bit like--not Rob Pattinson--but what I thought Edward might look like."

"You and every damned girl in school who read those books. I was in high school when they first came out." He narrowed his eyes. "Well, I'm not a damned sparkling vampire."

"No." She contained her giggles and took his hand as the door slid open at their floor. "Thank, God, you're a pain in the ass cowboy instead."

* * * *

Tired of being cooped up in the house and of thinking about Mike Ritter, Emily took a tablet, pen, and her guitar out to the porch. In a shady corner near the kitchen door, she sat in a wicker rocker and let her fingers play over the strings. Finding sound soothing to her nerves, she did it again, and let her instincts take over. The melody and lyrics flowed from her like a river, and as she repeated the chords and words, she jotted them on the music paper.

"Nice tune, though it's a bit too slow for my taste."

At the sound of the rough British voice, she jerked her head up to find her ex-husband leaning against a porch post as casually as if he belonged there. The barn and pasture framed his all-black attire and long jet hair. He lifted the cigarette he held between two long fingers, the black nail polish catching and absorbing the afternoon sunlight limning him in a weird sort of halo like some dark angel--or demon, more like it. The warm breeze wafted his exhaled smoke in her direction, causing her eyes to water and her belly take a flop. She'd always hated his stinking cigarettes.

Propping her guitar against the small table holding her tablet, she stood and squared her shoulders. "What the hell are you doing here?"

Her heart pounded as a slew of other questions bombarded her. How had he gotten this close to her? Where was EJ or Oliver and Jason? What if this had been Mike? She'd be dead. With a painful thud of her heart, she took a step back.

With a careless shrug, Fabian took another lazy puff on the cigarette. "I saw the interview the other night. I'm in Texas on tour with the band. Thought I'd drop in to see how you're doing. I noticed you have your bodyguards here--Oliver stopped me in the drive--and you're living with the sheriff?" His grin did nothing to hide the sarcasm. "How convenient for your safety from your deranged stepfather."

She fisted her hands, to keep them from shaking as much from anger as gut freezing fear. "Then you should see I'm fine."

After studying her for a moment, he snorted. "Bloody hell, you are."

She didn't miss the wrinkle of his long, aristocratic nose in disgust when he scanned the landscape and flicked ash into the shrubbery. For a foreigner who made his fortune in America, he didn't have much appreciation for anything outside New York City or LA. Not for the first time she wondered what the hell she'd seen in him.

"You never took stress well, and now that you're *rehabilitated*"--he matched the derisive tone on the last word with the same look that he'd given the countryside--"I'm sure you're having an even harder time of it."

Glaring at him, she tightened the grip she had on her fists. "You think I need drugs to get through this?"

"Don't you?" He took two steps toward her as he reached into a pocket of his jeans. His blue eyes softened as he touched her face with his other hand. She jerked away, and he smiled. "Come on, you know you miss me, red. You and I have something special."

When he feathered his fingers over her cheek again, she moved back, but with the furniture on one side and the porch railing on the other, she was effectively cornered.

"Something special? If you call getting high and fucking like animals special." Her voice came out as a high pitched squeak, and didn't sound anywhere near as disgusted as she wanted it to.

He shrugged and smiled. "You can't deny we had fun."

No, she couldn't, but it wasn't real, and after feeling bone deep love for a man, she never wanted anything else. Opening her mouth to tell him to go to hell, the words died on her tongue like dew in the hot wind. She gazed at the packet of white powder and licked her dry lips.

Sweet, much-needed oblivion.

"Take it." Fabian's low voice coaxed as if she were a beaten down dog. "You need it and there's not much here, but it should be enough to get you through this mess." He took another drag on his cigarette and blew out the smoke on the side of his mouth. "You could always come with me. The crazy bastard gunning for you won't find you."

When the arid stench drifted into her face, she didn't do more than blink. Feeling like Biblical Eve, she focused on the apple the demonic serpent dangled in front of her.

"Damn, you looked like shit on TV," the devil said.

"I'm pregnant."

He shrugged and looked her over. "You don't look it."

"But I am." The black and white image of the sonogram of her healthy, flourishing baby came to mind. Her new doctor had been pleased with her progress and moved her due date up three days to the sixth of October. "Aren't you afraid this will hurt the baby?" She wasn't sure who she was speaking to. Coke would harm her child, and she curled her left arm protectively around the mound of her baby girl. As if further reminding her mother of her existence the baby kicked hard enough to hurt, but Emily couldn't focus on anything other than the packet lying on his lily-white palm.

Again, he shrugged with an aloofness which struck Emily as painfully as an arctic ice storm. "This little bit won't hurt a thing. There's not more than a few lines here." He ran a hand through his long black hair. "Look, I don't know if what I feel for you is love. Hell, I don't know if I even believe in it. But I hate seeing you look this damned scared."

"I am scared." She swallowed against the lump in her throat. Her biggest fear lay in his hand. If she took what he offered, Mike would be the least of her worries. "I can't risk getting addicted again."

He scoffed in a loud disgusted noise. "I don't believe in that shit. A little coke won't hurt you."

This had always been his philosophy, and as fucked up as it was, she'd believed it too for a long time. She stared at the white packet lying in his palm. As if her arm wasn't connected to her brain, she lifted her hand and her fingers curled around the baggy of white powder.

* * * *

With the recent frustrating conversation with the FBI weighing heavy on his thoughts, EJ entered the kitchen, needing a cup of coffee. No one had seen Mike Ritter. How could a man, in these days of surveillance cameras at nearly every intersection of every two-bit town, disappear? Even McAllister had two such cameras at both of its traffic lights. The coffee finished, he added some milk and took a sip the strong brew.

At the thought of Mike, he moved toward the door onto the porch where Emily had taken her guitar. He didn't want to check up on her, he wanted to spend every second of every day with her. The implications made his heart leap. He'd never loved any woman as much as he did her, but fear of her rejection kept his mouth shut on the matter.

He heard the muffled voices from the porch when he opened the door. His stomach lurched with icy fear. Setting his coffee mug on the counter with a thump, he reached behind him with his other hand for the Glock he'd taken to wearing tucked into his belt. Had Mike shown up on his doorstep?

"That's right, love. After a little of this, you'll feel a whole lot better." At the British accent, a knife of jealousy stabbed through him, replacing some of the fear. Although EJ had never listened to the rocker's music, he knew exactly who the man was.

What the hell was Fabian McPhee doing on his porch?

"Please leave." Emily's strangled voice made her sound as if she'd been whipped.

EJ shifted to the side, which allowed him to see the figures and his heart clenched. McPhee leaned down and kissed Emily, and EJ's gut clenched when she didn't push him away or slap him. Was she kissing him back? The possibility sent a red hot brand through his heart. When McPhee stepped away, he spoke in a rough voice. "Call me if you need more."

EJ stepped into the shadows of the kitchen as the Brit turned to head off the porch. What would she do with the drugs? Hell, what would he do about them? As crazy as it sounded maybe arresting her for possession would be the best way to keep her and the baby safe.

He looked out at her. Emily faced the pasture, her profile pale and drawn.

Could he do that to her? Destroy her record and subject her to a trial in which she'd no doubt be convicted, destroying her career and taking her baby from her? No, he wouldn't, despite her feelings toward him. Maybe she'd give him the drugs, and he could destroy them. Should he ask her about them? With a shake of his head in answer to the question as much as to clear it from the sudden fog, he opened the door, then stepped out into the heat of the porch.

She turned suddenly as the flash of fear crossing her face disappeared, and he wondered if he'd imagined it. "I had a visitor."

"Oh." He stiffened his back and shoved his hands into his jeans pockets to keep them from shaking the confession from her. "Who?"

As she glanced out over the pasture where his twenty head of black Angus grazed, she said, "Fabian."

He fought to keep his voice steady. "What did he want?"

She shrugged and hugged her arms tightly around her body as if she were cold, in spite of the ninety-degree temperature reading for the day. He didn't see any sign of the small packet of cocaine. "To make sure I'm okay." Before he had a chance to speak, she picked up her guitar and brushed past him. "Please excuse me. I need to lie down. I'm not feeling well."

EJ turned to watch her hurry into the house and stared at the dark rectangle of the screen door for a long time. She never told him about the drugs, which meant one thing.

Emily intended to use them.

With a soul-cutting sigh, he sat down in the chair, the tablet on the table catching his attention. He picked it up, feeling numb and aching all at the same time, then read the lyrics written in a bold, rounded hand.

He set the tablet back on the table, closed his eyes, and swallowed hard enough to make his heart hurt.

Chapter 17

EJ never came to bed that night. Although Emily had no idea why he hadn't, she was happy for it. She sat up in EJ's king-sized bed and stared down at the packet of white powder. Although the stuff looked like harmless powdered sugar or cornstarch, she knew without tasting the coke it was of topnotch quality. Fabian always bought the best product. Where he got his supply, she didn't know. Cutting it with cornstarch would stretch the amount by possibly two or three days and would weaken it, too.

She could still escape from the fear and everything else if she cut it, but maybe the effect on the baby wouldn't be bad. Her mouth was dry and her stomach rumbled. When was the last time she'd drunk or eaten anything? The answer eluded her, simply because she didn't care. All she wanted was to rip open the packet and feel the sweet oblivion a few sniffs of the powder would give her.

Shivering despite the sheen of sweat slicking her skin, she pulled her knees up as far as she could. The bulge of her belly reminded her she wasn't alone in this decision. Wrapping her arms around her folded legs, she laid her head on her knees and sobbed. Her baby would hurt if she gave into the strangling addiction, but her daughter and she weren't the only victims. Her parents would be devastated, and her little brother, who idolized her as if she were a mythical goddess come to life, was old enough to be influenced by her bad decisions. He was the same age as their father when his mother had overdosed on pills and booze. His mother's death shaped Daddy's life in devastating ways, and hers when Mike Ritter used her father's messed-up emotions about his mother to manipulate him into leaving Momma. The thought caused her breath to hitch painfully in her throat.

Not that she planned to overdose, but if she became addicted again, what difference would it make? She'd have to leave which would break little Johnny's heart.

Her family weren't the only ones who would be disappointed in her.

The lyrics to the song she'd written on the porch rushed back to her. EJ. Every thought of the man made her stomach flutter. She loved him with a passion beyond anything she'd ever experienced. Whether he loved her or not, she didn't know, didn't dare speculate, but he did care for her. He definitely felt lust for her, but there was something tender there, too. The memories of all the nights she'd fallen to sleep in his embrace, his hand resting protectively over her daughter, came to mind.

She swallowed again against the bitter lump choking her. Even if EJ didn't love her now, she didn't doubt he was falling for her. Craving his love was wrong, but deep down in her soul she did.

With a wince, she stretched her legs out and placed her hands on the rounding of her belly. As she stared down at the basketball like curve, she caught sight of the packet of coke. EJ had shown more tenderness and fatherly concern, if not love, to her baby than the man who had created her. Fabian might not believe in addiction, but he couldn't deny the damage drugs had been proven to have on newborn babies. How could he show up here with that bag of poison if he cared even a little for their baby? He hadn't even asked about the child, only telling her she'd looked like shit.

Why had he given her the drugs? What was his end game?

The questions hadn't even been fully formed before she knew their answers. He wanted to control her. Fabian had never hit her, he never forbade her to do anything, but he'd destroyed her spirit as surely as if he'd smacked her around on a daily basis.

She reached out with a shaking hand and touched the cool plastic covering the viciously taunting powder. Did she honestly want that man to ever be near her baby girl?

The question startled her more than the answer did. She'd been keeping EJ at arms' length because of some ideal fantasy Fabian would someday want to be a father, but today he showed his true self. He wasn't worthy of the name.

With a deep, cleaning breath, she snatched up the packet and crawled off the bed. No, Fabian McPhee wasn't more than a sperm donor. He would never be like her father. She hoped EJ was the man destined to be her baby's father.

She entered the en suite bathroom and met her swollen, bloodshot eyes. Tears she hadn't noticed ran down her white and red splotched cheeks. She did look like shit; she'd never appeared more devastated, and she'd never been stronger.

Careful not to spill the fine powder, she opened the ziplock of the baggie. Inhaling deeply with a breath heavily scented with EJ's spicy soap, she turned the plastic over and watched dispassionately as several hundred dollars of highest-grade cocaine fell into the toilet, coating the water in the bowl before settling on the bottom of the porcelain. Once the bag was empty, except for a fine coating, she turned to the sink, filled the packet with water, and washed the substance down the drain.

"What kept you from using the coke?"

EJ's deep voice was pitched low, causing her to nearly miss the question. She met his gaze in the mirror above the vanity. He stood in the opening of the door.

"A lot of things." She sighed, then glanced down at the toilet as she pushed the lever to flush. A thrill ran through her as she realized the craving for the drug was replaced with a new determination she'd never had until now. Before the twirling water even had a chance to empty the bowl, she turned and smiled at him. "You mostly."

"Me?"

She leaned against the edge of the sink and a quiver of deep need settled low in her belly at the sight of him. His short blond hair stood up in places as if he'd repeatedly been running his fingers through the thick mass. The expanse of muscular chest and shoulders were tanned a light brown from working his ranch without a shirt on, reminding her of the boy she'd spent her teenage years daydreaming about. Above his heart, the Army tattoo of an eagle with an American flag in his talons couldn't let her forget the brave man he'd grown into. Springy, dark golden hair covered his pectorals and formed a line between his six-pack to disappear in the open fly of soft, low-riding jeans. He was gorgeous and always had been. Her old girlish crush melded into the emotions she now had for him, and her heart ached from the joy.

"I love you." Her voice was rough from lack of sleep and the tears she'd shed. He widened his eyes, and the way his breath hitched encouraged her to tell him everything. "I think I've always loved you. I used to follow you around the ranch wishing you'd wait for me to grow up. You were and always had been my fantasy. Every love song I've ever written has been about you." She laughed, the sound hoarse and scratchy. "Remember that summer you came home and I was between tour dates?" She didn't give him time to answer as the memory of riding with him through the pastures came back to mind. "I'm surprised you didn't see through my awkward flirting. God, I was smitten with you. Then when we brought the horses back to the barn, you kissed me on the cheek and told me to behave myself. I watched you leave that barn holding my cheek and smiling like a fool. I carved your initials in the doorframe of the barn to mark the spot where you kissed me. Dad thought they were mine because my middle name is Josephina and never questioned them." Again she laughed, but this time it was even shakier than before. If he remembered any of it, he wasn't giving her a clue. "I wrote *My Summertime Lover* that night. It's my fantasy of what I wished would have happened in the pasture." Unable to take the wide-eyed way he stood there staring at her, she swallowed hard. Had she completely scared him away with her rambling? "Please say something."

In a heartbeat, he enveloped her in an embrace, picked her up off her feet, and covered her lips in a sweet, deep kiss. He tasted of mint, coffee, and passion. After a moment, he pulled out of the kiss and rested his forehead on hers. His pewter eyes were clear and bright, and she swore she could see into his soul. The depth of the emotion she saw in his gaze rushed over her like a tidal wave, washing away the last visages of any lingering cravings for coke. All she'd ever want was him.

"God, I love you, Emily." His deep voice rasped the words as if he'd run a marathon. "I think deep down I've been waiting for you to grow up since I first laid eyes on you. I know it seems crazy, but something has always drawn me to you." He kissed her again, then pulled back enough to whisper, "I love your baby girl, too. I know she'll never be mine, but I hope you'll let me stand in as Daddy to her."

"If you let me stand in for Momma to Austin."

He smiled and nodded. "I wouldn't have it any other way."

She held him close, and shivered at the intensity of his words. "EJ, you are everything I've ever wanted. Make love to me."

He lifted her and she wrapped her legs around his waist. As she buried her fingers into his hair, she pressed her lips to his and kissed him. Sweeping his tongue into her mouth, he turned up the passion as he carried her to the bed. He set her on the mattress and pulled her tank top over her head. She wasn't wearing a bra, and he immediately leaned down to suck one of the hard, sensitive nipples.

She let out a long groan at the tingling need shooting through her to settle between her legs as he suckled her. When he moved to the other breast, she reached for his jeans. Together they pushed them down his legs and he kicked them away, then they got rid of her shorts. Within a few heartbeats they were naked, and he leaned over her.

Breathing heavy, he kissed her and skimmed his hand over her belly down to her mound. She sucked in a breath and arched her back when his fingers slipped over the needy nerves at her center.

"You're wet," he whispered in the ear he nibbled. "I can't wait."

When he slipped a finger inside her as his thumb caressed circles around her clit, she moaned and gripped his shoulders. "Then don't."

He shifted to bring his body in line with hers, and she wrapped her legs around his back. With a sure thrust, he entered her and within a few pumps she was cresting. The orgasm came hard and fast, but had never been sweeter. She opened her eyes to him watching her with eyes full of awe and love her body heated from it. As his thrusts quickened and deepened, perspiration shimmered over his tanned skin in the dim light of the bedroom. His hair was mussed and the dark stubble of beard covered his high angular cheeks and strong square chin. As he gritted his teeth and his muscles and sinews corded in his neck and shoulders with his control, he never looked more beautiful.

The coil of pleasure tightened deep in her lower belly and she cried out when it snapped. He slammed into her, stilled, and with a roar, broke apart with her.

When they came back together, she knew he'd given her part of his soul and he had hers.

* * * *

With her hands resting on the growing mound of her belly, Emily sat on the porch and stared unseeing out over the pasture. The sun was high in the sky and the day was hot, but she needed to be outside. Last night's mental torture then the relief of the early morning's confessions and passion had left her drained, but she couldn't relax. They'd made love twice before drifting to sleep as dawn lightened the eastern sky outside the large windows.

The joy from sharing in EJ's love had evaporated when his cellphone rang at a little after nine this morning. A car matching the description of the one belonging to Mike's accomplice had been found abandoned this side of the McAllister County line, twenty-five miles north of town. The body of Brooklyn Jensen was found stuffed in the trunk. She'd been shot in the head, and had been dead for at least three days.

Emily shivered and wrapped her arms around herself. EJ hadn't wanted to leave her, but he had no choice. He had to oversee the investigation until the Texas Rangers and FBI showed up. She'd promised him she'd stay inside until he could spare a deputy to send out to the ranch, but she needed some air. Her nerves were shot. Both Oliver and Jason patrolled the yard. She should have felt safe with their presence, but she didn't.

Mike was in town and wanted her dead.

The sound of a gunshot cracked the still air like a pin to a balloon. She stood, but couldn't make her legs move. She couldn't even let the trapped scream out. Tingles of shock and fear numbed her limbs. Paralyzed by the scene, she couldn't do anything but watch as Oliver fell, like a tree struck down by an ax, at the edge of the yard. Jason crouched behind a garden shed and fired in the direction where the killing shot had been fired, but the murderer didn't show himself.

A return shot came from the direction of the barn.

"Emily! Get the hell inside the house and call Cowley!" Jason's nasally New England accent got through the fog in her head.

She ran into the house and grabbed her cellphone from the counter. Her hands shook, causing her to drop the slippery iPhone twice before finally hitting the correct button to call EJ's phone. With her heart beating hard enough from fear to make her chest hurt, she stared out the window behind the kitchen table. As she listened to EJ's phone ring, she held her breath when Jason made a run for the house in a crouch, using trees and little Austin's big plastic playhouse for cover. When he reached the porch, another shot was fired from the barn. Jason's eyes widened and he dropped to his knees. She screamed as EJ greeted her, and she dropped the phone again.

Her legs were unable to hold her upright, and she crumbled to the floor where she fumbled with the phone. The thump of her heart nearly drowned out EJ's frantic voice calling her name. Holding the cell in both hands, she put it to her ear. Before she could get her mouth to form words, the kitchen door crashed open, and in the opening, silhouetted by the bright sunlight, stood Mike Ritter.

The gash of his malicious grin showed absurdly white in his dark beard. "Hello, *daughter*."

"Mike," she squeaked before dropping the phone again. This time she didn't get the chance to pick it up.

Dressed in dirty jeans and a ripped flannel shirt over a filthy undershirt, Mike moved toward her. She made a grab for the phone as it emitted EJ yelling for her to tell him what was happening. The terror in his voice was as tangible as her own fear. Mike set his boot heel on the fragile glass front of the iPhone and smashed it, effectively shutting off EJ and her link to the only man she trusted to keep her safe.

Mike grunted and looked down at her. His hair was longer than she'd ever seen it and his eyes held the gleam of a fanatic. The malice of the grin slashing through the unkempt beard added to his appearance of complete madness. "I don't think we're going to bother the sheriff with this little reunion."

With a clarity at odds with the numbing tingling of her rubbery limbs, she watched as Mike shifted the rifle to hit her with the butt. As pain exploded in her head she thought of EJ and her baby girl, then the world slipped into utter blackness.

Chapter 18

EJ had experienced bone-melting terror a few times in his life. The kind of fear that turned his guts to icy water, and had him shivering from the frozen knowledge of impotence. Yet beads of prickly sweat broke out over his skin, as if the ice was pushing all the heat from his body.

When Emily's phone went dead, he thought he'd die from the knowledge he'd been played like the fucking fool he was.

Mike had known EJ would have to leave Emily to conduct an investigation of the dead body he'd placed well away from where she was.

"Emily!" he yelled into his phone, knowing she was gone. "Fuck!" He balled his fist and hit the hood of the dead woman's car hard enough to put a satisfying dent in the dirty blue hood. Too damned bad it wasn't Mike Ritter's face. He inhaled a painful breath and turned to the startled gazes of his deputies, two FBI agents, and the Texas Ranger. Fighting for air to fill his constricted lungs, he grabbed his hat off his head and ran his throbbing hand through his hair.

Clint Grier stepped away from the coroner and rounded the Toyota Camry. "What happened?"

EJ jammed his hat back on his head and headed toward his Tahoe. "Mike Ritter has Emily."

"Holly shit." Clint didn't try to stop him as EJ pushed past him.

"EJ? You can't leave the scene yet," Coroner Scott Lewis said as he passed the body of Brooklyn Jensen.

As he opened the door of his SUV, EJ glared at his old high school classmate. Scott had always been a stickler for rules even back in school. "I don't fucking care. This woman is dead. I would bet my ranch Mike Ritter murdered her. I don't need any more evidence." He got behind the wheel. "But I do need to find him." *Before he kills the woman I love and our baby.*

Slamming the door, he turned the ignition. At the same time, the passenger door opened and Clint Grier climbed in.

"What do you think you're doing?" EJ scowled at his lieutenant. "You need to stay here."

"Like hell. You need someone to watch your back and to make sure you don't do anything stupid. I know you have a personal stake in going after Mike." Clint buckled his seatbelt before looking at EJ with a hard line to his jaw and a dark hatred in his eyes. "I do too. I may not have the woman I care about at stake, but he made a fool out of me. I should have put a bullet in Mike Ritter's head eight years ago." His voice pitched low with a dangerous edge. "I won't make that mistake again."

EJ would feel the same if he'd worked with Mike Ritter and had been his lieutenant for over ten years but had no idea of his illegal activities.

"You may have to wait your turn." EJ shoved the rig into gear with a hard shove and hit the siren. "That bastard is mine."

A few moments later, Clint asked, "What happened?"

EJ shook his head as he watched the miles of flat ranchland crawl by. He was pushing the Tahoe as fast as he dared on the two-lane county road. Nothing would be gained if he wrapped them around a telephone pole in his recklessness. But damn, the miles seemed to take forever to cross. "Emily called, but I never actually spoke with her. She must have dropped the phone a few times, and what I did hear…" He trailed off and shook his head. "Mike has her."

"Damn." Clint's tone told EJ he knew as well as him what they might find back at the ranch. "Where are her bodyguards?"

"I don't know." EJ glanced at his partner. Clint's face had gone completely white. "If Mike has a gun, then they're probably dead."

Clint took a deep breath and let it out slowly. "The bastard set us up."

EJ nodded and looked out the side window at the endless flatness of pasture dotted with cattle and horses. A few trees broke up the landscape here and there. At the intersection, he turned right onto River Road, which led to his ranch. "Yes. He made sure the sheriff's department would be occupied chasing its tail."

Although he was glad for the older man's help in a fight, he didn't want to talk. As if sensing his mood, Clint kept his thoughts to himself. EJ turned into his driveway with a growing ball of ice in his gut.

"Look." Clint pointed out the window. "Is that one of Emily's guards?"

EJ slammed on the breaks and threw the SUV into park. "Yeah."

Without another word EJ got out of the Tahoe, pulling his Glock and looked at Clint. The older man had the radio in his hand and called the county dispatch. He should have called for backup long before now, but he'd been holding onto the fragile strand of hope that Oliver and Jason could handle Mike.

He crouched and hurried to the still form of the big man. With a silent prayer, he felt for a pulse at his thick neck. The beat was slow, but surprisingly strong. He might live if given the proper medical care. The sight of the wound wasn't readily visible amid Oliver's black t-shirt and jeans, but he smelled the pungent odor of copper and searched for some sign. He found the sticky blood at the man's side. A small hole in his shirt cued him in where the bullet entered.

"He's alive," he called over his shoulder toward the SUV and Clint. "Call for an ambulance."

He didn't wait for Clint to respond, but brought his gun up in the ready position, and ran toward the house. At the sight of Jason Harmon lying face down at the back door, EJ's heart thudded harder in this chest. Blood stained dark on the back of his t-shirt. EJ leaned down and searched for a pulse at his neck and let out his breath when he found one. It was slow and skipped beats, but it was there. He looked over his shoulder at Clint by the SUV where he was talking on the radio. "Clint, have two ambulances sent. Jason's alive too, but barely."

EJ shook from the fear of what might lay behind the closed door. The sweat trickling down his face and backbone had nothing to do with the heat as a chill sent a shiver through him. Was Emily lying in a pool of her own blood behind the door? He took a deep breath that seemed to get stuck in his throat and opened the door, his finger on the trigger of the Glock as he forced himself to take a cautious step into the dark interior.

When he found nothing amiss in the kitchen except for a tumbled chair and Emily's crushed cellphone. He rushed through the house, looking in every room and closet. He met Clint in the living room. The fear crippling him on the porch at what he'd find before he entered the house turned into choking panic as he looked at Clint. "She's not here. Oh, Jesus, he's taken her."

* * * *

Awareness came back to Emily with a sickening ache in her right temple and a swift kick to her bladder from the inside. She lifted her hand to touch the throbbing spot on her head, but couldn't move her arm. Stinging pain banded her wrist. She must be bound. When she tried to move her legs, they also found the resistance of biting, rough rope. She swallowed against the bile the movement caused to rush up and slowly opened her eyes. The right one was glued shut, like the time she had conjunctivitis as a kid. After a moment of panic, she determined when Mike hit her with the gun stock he broke the skin and blood had run into her eye and dried. This idea didn't make the situation any less frightening, but at least she was able to think clearly, despite the obvious concussion.

A spurt of static sounded from the far corner. Some kind of radio? When an authoritative woman's voice came from the corner, she narrowed her eye and concentrated on her words, soon discerning the radio was a police scanner. No wonder Mike had been able to stay one step ahead of the cops.

Her left eye focused, and she looked around the best she could with that side of her face smashed against the rough wood plank floor and the dimness of the room. She didn't lift her head out of fear of drawing attention to herself and because even the thought of moving made her head throb.

The stink of mustiness and age from the dark, dirty floor she lay on filled her nostrils and choked her until she switched to breathing through her mouth. A rough-made wood table and two benches stood directly in front of her. To her left was a window covered with what looked like half a holey feed sack. Next to the window sat a small, old-fashioned potbelly stove; to her right against the wall was a thin mattress on a metal cot. Shifting her hands to the wall behind her, she found unfinished planks. She ventured to turn her head. The room was dim in the corners as if the feeble light couldn't puncture the dark. From the heavy stench of kerosene, she assumed the source of light came from the ancient lantern on the table. The windows on either side of the plank door were also covered with mouse-nibbled burlap. A large ten-point buck head mounted on the wall above as if it was keeping guard with its wide, glass eyes. Her heart jumped into her throat.

She was at the cabin deep in the interior of the Double K. Accessible by horseback or ATV, the hunting cabin had been built by her great-grandfather. She'd been to the small place a few times, but its remoteness kept the cabin mostly forgotten except during deer season, and since she abhorred the thought of killing hapless animals for sport, she never had a reason to come.

How the hell had she gotten out here?

Tired of lying on the hard floor and needing to know what was going on, she closed her eye, braced against the stab of pain sure to come with the movement and twisted herself into a sitting position against the wall. A wave of dizzying nausea hit her hard enough to take her breath as a blast of pain shot through her skull. She fought the urge to throw up, took a long slow breath through her nose, then opened her eye when the dizziness subsided.

From this vantage point, she got a better look at the room making up the whole of the cabin. An old sideboard sat in the corner. On its top sat a battered enamel basin and various cans of soups and meats, along with several loaves of bread. Three full and two empty gallon jugs of water sat next to an ancient camp-style coffee pot. Food provisions? How long had Mike been holed up here?

She had no idea what time it was. Hell, she didn't know what day it was. A fly landed on her blood-encrusted forehead. She shook the nasty thing off, ignoring the pain that knifed through her head with the motion. Over the irritated buzzing of the insect, a horse whinnied outside. Mike must have brought her here on horseback. The mechanics of which she didn't want to think on too hard considering she was pregnant and had been unconscious. He must have left EJ's ranch by way of the pastures, crossed his parents' Circle R Ranch, then Tucker Cowley's place, and finally most of the Double K to reach the cabin. That trip would have taken hours on a horse as none of the ranches were less than three hundred acres. Mike wouldn't have wanted to be seen by anyone either.

When the door opened, she saw the sky was black. Night then. She flinched as her captor stepped into the room. He sat a bucket of water on the floor next to her. He must have gotten it from the creek running near the cabin. With the harsh shadows cast by the pale yellow glow of the lantern, Mike Ritter looked like a deranged mountain man. A hysterical giggle bubbled to the surface at this. The closest mountain--hell, the closest hill--was over a hundred miles away. McAllister County, Texas, was as flat as sheet of paper.

He rummaged in a duffle bag on the cot and pulled out a threadbare cloth. She strangled back the urge to laugh as he knelt beside her. Only his eyes were discernible. His face was in complete shadow. Wrinkling her nose at the foul odors of unwashed body and horse sweat, she turned her head to the side, as much to escape the smell as the craziness in his bloodshot eyes.

"Glad to see you're awake. I was beginning to think I'd killed you." He dipped the rag into the bucket and wrung out the excess water.

She about gagged on the stench of his breath, but forced herself to meet his bright brown eyes. "Isn't that what you want to do to me?"

He shrugged, and the side of his mouth showed teeth as he grinned, then he dabbed the cold cloth on her wound. "Yes. But the timing depends on how much trouble you cause me."

Sara Walter Ellwood

She flinched, more from his touch than from pain, and fought down the growing hysteria by grasping onto the fact he hadn't killed her--yet. As long as she was alive, EJ had time to figure out where she was, or she could find a way to get away from him.

"You're living with the sheriff." He grabbed hold of her chin and forced her toward him as he cleaned the blood off her face. His cold eyes narrowed as he looked pointedly at the mound of her belly her tank top did little to hide. "You can't be that far along. Is he the father?"

Unable to move away from his surprisingly tender touch, she stared into his eyes and for a beat they didn't belong to a deranged stranger, but instead to the man she once loved as her daddy. An uncomfortable pinch of grief twisted her heart. She didn't know why he asked, but she considered her answer. True, most people would have been surprised to know she was seven months pregnant based on the size of her baby bump, although she'd grown considerably larger in the past two weeks. Her doctor had told her she'd most likely grow fast in the last trimester.

Why had she been adamant about not entertaining the thought of EJ stepping in as father to her baby? Had the reason been about preventing her daughter the same confusion she'd had? Sure Fabian could come into her little girl's life and suddenly want to be her father, but she'd always know about him. Emily was divorced, and although Fabian was abusive and manipulative, her ex hadn't tricked her as Mike had her mother and father.

When the real reason for not wanting EJ to make a claim on her baby hit her, she gasped. If Mike hadn't manipulated Momma into marrying him, if her father had honestly not wanted her mother, Mike would still be in Emily's life. Most likely she'd still call him Daddy and would still love him as such. She wanted to protect her baby not from Fabian coming back and wanting to be a father, but from the pain of losing the man she would undoubtedly love as Daddy.

But EJ was nothing like Mike, and on the flip side, Fabian was nothing like Seth. Fabian honestly didn't want his child. His demanding she take the cocaine the other day proved that. EJ loved her baby. He'd shown her how much at her OB appointment. During the sonogram, he'd held her hand and stared at the monitor showing a black and white shadow of her baby while an utterly awed expression came over his handsome face. It was the face of a father, and it was about time she acknowledged it.

She lifted her chin and gazed into the eyes of the man who had never been her father. She may have loved him as such, but Mike Ritter had never truly loved her or her mother. "My ex-husband was the sperm donor, but her father is EJ Cowley."

With a snort of harsh laughter, Mike stood and dropped the bloody cloth in the bucket. "Her? Well, too bad neither man is going to meet his daughter."

His words shuddered through her making her cold to the bone. "What are you going to do to me?"

Laughing, he picked up the bucket, went to the door, and tossed the water outside, then set the pail on the floor. Without turning, he spoke in a low, deadly calm tone as if they were discussing the weather. "I'm going to kill you, but maybe not as soon as I'm done with you." What did he mean? He looked over his shoulder at her. "I've decided to not be hasty in my revenge. The brat will help me get the hell out of this country."

The ruthless, ugly smile he gave her as he stepped toward her sent ice through her, and she tried to shrink as far against the wall as possible. She wrapped her arms around her knees, wanting to protect her baby. "What are you going to do to us?"

He leaned down and grabbed her arm, pulling her to her feet. The sudden change in position sent a stab of pain through her head, and his sour smell turned her stomach. He pressed her against the wall, bringing the whole length of his body against her, when she felt the telltale ridge pressing against her belly, she wanted to scream and tried to twist away, but with her dizziness and the bindings on her limbs, she couldn't even move.

His lips were close to her ear and his hot breath burned her skin. "You've become a beautiful woman, Emily. I must have jacked off a thousand times while looking at one of your magazine pictures." The image he conjured made her gag, but if he noticed, he ignored her and went on, "You know the real reason I cheated on your mother with Tammy Jo McAllister?"

She stared into his crazy, bloodshot, brown eyes and shivered.

He shifted her to the cot and pushed her down onto the filthy mattress. As he shrugged out of his shirt, he said, "You." Her surprise must have shown through her utter horror. "I never was sexually attracted to your mother. God, I could barely get a hard on around her. It was too much like fucking my sister."

Her mother had told her much of the same thing once that her marriage to Mike had not only been loveless, but sexless as well.

He tossed his shirt on the floor and pulled off his undershirt. As he resumed his sickening speech, he reached for her hands. "You were eleven then. A beautiful girl, and I wanted you." He unbound her hands, but before she could even think of fighting, he retied her wrists to the metal bed frame above her head. "I had to find a woman to take my mind off you. I may have sold girls who ended up being someone's sex toys, but I couldn't risk making you mine. Tammy Jo presented herself. She was still beautiful and as rich as King Midas. I took her up on her offer. Besides, your mother's money was running out. I couldn't touch any more of it."

He smiled that ugly grin again and feathered his fingers over the side of her face. She flinched her head to the side, and he snorted. "I used to stand in your doorway when you'd come to stay with Tammy Jo and me, and I'd watch you sleep." He gave her a sly grin. "Then when I fucked her, I pretended she was you. Her baby was conceived after one of those times."

When he reached for the rope on her feet, a terror more devastating than dying numbed her senses. He untied her feet. She fought him by kicking and stabbing with her bare heels, until he punched her in the swollen mound of her baby daughter. She let out a scream of pain as hot tears burned her face. The nausea she'd been fighting since waking rushed up her throat. She turned her head and retched over and over, but since she hadn't eaten or drunk anything since that morning, nothing came up but bitter bile.

He stripped her of her shorts and panties, then tied her legs spread eagle to the bed frame. When he stood, he grabbed the front of her tank top and gave it a hard yank between his hands. The thin material gave away and ripped neatly down the center. He brushed his hands over the tops of her breasts, down the valley between to the clasp of her bra in the front. When he pushed the lacy cups aside, he sucked in a breath, then palmed her breasts.

After a moment of painfully pinching and fumbling her nipples, he stepped back and reached for his belt. His cold gaze pinned her to the bed as surely as the ties did. "I'm going to fuck you, Emily, until I'm tired of you. Then I'll decided if I want your brat or not."

She bit her lip and squeezed her eyes closed, waiting for the violation. Her uterus caught in a gripping cramp, making her groan. Had he hurt the baby when he punched her? If she could, she'd kill Mike Ritter.

When the back window shattered with a loud bang, she opened her eyes.

Chapter 19

The large map of McAllister County taunted EJ from the wall in his office. He'd studied the outline of town with its neat crisscross of streets and houses, and the large pastel shaded shapes, representing the tracts of land in the county. Green indicated state lands, pale blue showed the historical Rose Ranch once owned by the McAllister family. Yellow, pink, lavender, and orange represented the ranches, making the square county look like an Easter crazy patch quilt.

Where the hell could he have taken her?

Every road and street in the county was blocked. Not even an ant could cross the county line without notice. If his officers, the FBI, Texas Rangers, State Police, or the five county firefighters he'd deputized didn't block the roads, the neighboring counties had them shut down.

For at least the fiftieth time he traced a finger from the far northwest corner of the county where the car had been found that morning, to the Matheson's ranch two miles from the car where a horse, bridle, and saddle had been reported stolen three days ago. EJ scratched at the bristly beard growing in. He'd bet his ranch Ritter stole the horse, after dumping the car. But where in God's name did he go after that?

To his place and Emily. Oliver had wakened long enough before going into surgery to tell Clint Grier he'd seen a saddled horse by the barn and was going to investigate when he was shot. Jason was still in critical care, but was expected to live. Both men were. God, he prayed they survived. Emily would blame herself if either one of them died.

EJ traced the obscure trails from the Matheson Ranch to his own, circumventing the town and avoiding the main roads. It definitely was possible and probably could be done in a day of hard riding. Where had he been hiding out until this morning? He had to have been close enough to know when EJ had gotten the call the car had been found.

"Has the magic wall told you anything yet? You've been staring at that thing for an hour."

EJ turned to Clint Grier standing in his doorway. "Maybe." He proceeded to tell Clint about his thoughts. Circling the ranches out on River Road, he said, "He's holed up here somewhere."

Clint narrowed his eyes and rubbed the back of his neck. "I already checked out the Ritter ranch. He's not there. The old line cabin he'd used to house the illegals he'd filtered through the county was torn down after his arrest eight years ago. No one on the Circle R has heard from him either."

EJ twisted his mouth up in thought and stared at the ranches he'd encompassed in his invisible outline: the Ritter's Circle R, his place, his brothers' spreads, and the Double K. He didn't have any line shacks. His uncle had torn them down years ago. Neither did his brothers' ranches.

He tapped his finger on the yellow shape representing the Double K. The ranch didn't have any line cabins either, but a memory lurked in the corner of his mind like a spider in a web. With numb fingers, he pulled his cell from its clip on his belt and hit the number for Tucker's phone.

Two rings later and without preamble, his brother snapped, "Did you find her?"

"No." EJ held Clint's gaze as the other man waited. "Hey, do you know if the Kendalls still use that old hunting cabin in the northwest corner?"

"Yeah, it's still there. Seth isn't much of a hunter, but Vince and I have used it to watch deer."

A million thoughts clamored in his brain. Could Mike make it this easy to find him? Or had he been hoping hiding in plain sight would make him invisible? A shudder went through EJ. The bastard almost fooled them. "Thanks, bro."

Tucker asked, "Is that where you think he's keeping Emily? EJ, the only way to get back there is on horseback or ATV."

"I'm hoping that's where he is. Saddle five good horses for hard riding and have two of the flat-bedded ATVs gassed up, too. Have them ready in twenty minutes, Tuck." He hung up and put his phone back on his belt, then grabbed his hat off his desk. "C'mon. I want five of the best riders we have in the department and two EMTs to meet me at the Double K."

* * * *

The ride over the Double K was taking longer than he'd hoped. The ranch was seven hundred acres of flat pastures and hay fields, but the cabin had been built near a creek in a thick grove of ponderosa pines, hackberry trees, and a ton of underbrush. Cutting across the pastures in the darkening evening, with only the light from the headlights on the ATVs guiding them had been hard, but now that they reached the grove, EJ reined in. The cabin was a good five hundred yards away, but they'd have to walk in or risk being heard. He swung out of the saddle of his borrowed horse and went to the ATVs. The two EMTs watched him approaching.

"We can't go any farther," George Wallace said when EJ stopped beside the slight man of about fifty. "I thought your brother said there's a path to the cabin."

"There is, but here we can hide the horses and go in on foot. I want you both to stay here until I radio you." He pointed to the south. "Follow the edge of the grove until you get to a trail. About fifty feet. You can't miss it."

George glanced into the dark in the south and frowned. "Okay. Dave and I will stay here until we hear from you."

EJ clapped him on the shoulder. "Thanks."

His men dismounted and tethered their mounts on low branches of the trees, then they silently followed EJ through the brambles toward the cabin. Afraid that Mike would either have the trail booby-trapped or be watching it, he advised a plan to approach the cabin from the windowless side, then circle around. The going was tedious and his heart ached with each agonizingly slow step. What if Mike had already killed her?"

What if his lack of actual planning got her and his men killed?

He pushed the questions out of his head the best he could and focused on pushing through the underbrush.

"Hey, do you see that?" Clint asked in a low voice by his side.

EJ peered through the thicket and his heart leapt to his throat. He pulled his Glock and fingered the trigger. A silhouette of a man came from the creek side of the cabin carrying what looked like a bucket onto the porch. Tethered to the side of the porch was a horse, directly in line of him and Ritter. He sighted down the gun, itching to take a shot, but he couldn't risk missing or hitting the horse. When the door opened, dim, yellow light illuminated him for a moment before darkness swallowed the porch again when he disappeared in the cabin. EJ let out the breath he was holding and lowered the gun.

"Damn, wish we had a clear shot." Clint ground out the words as he lowered his own Glock then spat on the dark ground.

"I know." He patted his lieutenant's shoulder and turned in a crouch toward his other three deputies. "I can't remember if this thing has a back door or not, but I'm sure it has a window. Bucky and Billy, the two of you go around back. Shoot the bastard on sight if you get him in your crosshairs. Understand?" Whether or not, they could see the hatred in his face, he didn't know, but he poured more than enough into the last word. The deputies nodded and didn't question his order. Glancing at Clint and Deputy Joe Kinkaid, he said, "The three of us are going through the front door."

EJ heard the sounds of what may have been a scuffle inside and the cry of pain from a woman--from Emily. With as much speed as the undergrowth and the years of dry leaves would allow, they half ran, half crawled to the front of the cabin.

He motioned for Joe to stay put and to cover them if need be, then he and Clint pulled their guns and bounded the last yards for the porch. When a shot rang through the night from behind, EJ's heart leapt into his throat. Was Ritter dead? In the low light from the windows and the full moon above, he and Clint looked at each other as they settled against the wall on either side of the door between the curtained rectangles. Clint nodded, and EJ reached for the doorknob.

"I'll kill her if anyone out there makes another move." A rifle shot and a scream from Emily, followed by loud sobbing, punctuated the words.

"Bucky. Billy. Do you copy?" Clint called out to the two deputies in the back of the cabin on his radio pinned to his shoulder.

"Billy's been shot." Bucky McCoy's call over the radio clipped by EJ's ear stopped him from barging into the cabin. "He's okay--shoulder shot. We're pulling back out of line of fire."

"Roger. Billy, if you can get back to the medics, go." Clint answered when EJ didn't.

"I'm okay," Billy said with an air of defiance. "A glancing shot. I had him in my sights, but damn, he must have seen me or something, because he shifted enough that I missed him and he got me."

They had to stay to the shadows. The moon was high enough to give off enough light for Ritter to see through the holes in the burlap. EJ fisted his hand on the door handle and swallowed the bile rushing up his throat. He was as much a prisoner as Emily. If he barged in, he'd either get Emily killed or one of his men, but how could he do nothing?

He turned toward the window by his other side. The thing was covered with burlap, but he found a hole and peered into the cabin. A gasp ripped out of his throat when he saw Emily tied naked to a cot. He stopped breathing when he saw the blood between her thighs. Oh, Christ was she hurt? Had the bastard raped her?

What he could see of her face was pinched as her body undulated as much as her bindings would allow. "EJ! Help! Oh, God," she gasped in pain. "I think I'm losing the baby."

The sight of her sent a cold spear of determination though him. He searched the visible cabin for Ritter, but the hole didn't allow him to see much.

"Shut the fuck up, bitch!" Ritter's words were as frigid as an arctic wind. "Or, I'll put a bullet in your head."

Emily let out another sobbing groan. If he didn't make a move, Emily and her baby would die. But if he did... He couldn't think of the what-ifs.

Motioning for Joe to come up on the porch, he pressed his back against the other side of the window, his gun held up in the ready. EJ pointed to the stacked firewood between the end porch post and the wall of the cabin and gestured to the two windows, then whispered, "On three."

Joe and Clint nodded understanding. Clint picked up two chunks of the wood and took his place against the door again. EJ turned toward Joe and jerked his head toward Clint's side. "Cover me from the other side of the window," he whispered. "Draw off his fire. Clint, you open the door once I shoot the son of a bitch."

Joe nodded and ducked below the glow to come up on the far side of Clint's window.

God, he hoped to heaven and hell this worked. Holding up his Glock with his finger hovering on the trigger, he whispered, "Three, two, one!"

Clint tossed the heavy chunks of wood into the windows on either side of the door, breaking glass and pulling the flimsy coverings off. Joe shot into the room, while EJ sought out Mike down the barrel of his gun. Ritter hid behind the turned-up table in the far corner with the sideboard to his back. EJ didn't have much of a target, but then he didn't need one. The top of Ritter's head popped up as he aimed at Joe. He must have seen EJ and turned to fire at Emily at the same time EJ pulled the trigger.

The combined racket of gunshots going off in close range was nearly drowned out by the screams from the bed.

Chapter 20

Sweet Jesus, she was tiny.

EJ peered through the plate glass window separating the visitor's gallery and the newborn intensive care unit. Cadence Susanna lay in an incubator on a pink blanket. Her name was bigger than she was. He snorted at the thought. The diaper seemed to swallow her scrawny body. The doctor said she weighed two pounds, three ounces and was thirteen inches long. Her legs and arms appeared not much bigger than the numerous tubes and wires attached to her.

God, she was beautiful.

Please give her strength.

His heart seized as he silently prayed that she survive. He had a horrible fear her small life would disappear, despite the assurances from the pediatric specialist taking care of his daughter that she was healthy and had a better chance than most premature babies.

Emily would be okay. She'd gone into early labor, most likely brought on from the stresses of the day and the injuries she'd sustained to her abdomen. Her labor had started after the fucking bastard had punched her. The sight of her tied naked, battered, and bloody to the filthy cot would haunt him for the rest of his life. He'd untied her and wrapped a blanket around her, praying to heaven she hadn't been raped. At the memories, EJ swallowed the bitter satisfaction that he'd shot the son of a bitch dead.

He shook all thought of those horrible minutes from the time he shot Ritter, to him carrying Emily out of the cabin and looked to the future. As soon as Emily was discharged and Cadence was out of danger, he planned to ask her to marry him.

"Is she going to live?"

He turned at the British accented voice and stiffened his spine. Fabian McPhee stood next to him, his hands shoved into the pockets of his black leather coat.

"Yes." He looked back at the rock star and forced the fists at his sides to relax. Punching the SOB wouldn't do anyone any good.

McPhee squinted in at the baby. "What are all those tubes coming out of her?"

"Life support." EJ's shoulders sagged as he stared at the baby. Emily's parents arrived at the Amarillo hospital at about the same time Fabian had, but it was EJ who'd stayed with Emily while she delivered the baby. He'd held Emily's hand and poured his strength into her, fighting his own fears and heartache that her--their--baby wouldn't survive. "She isn't able to breathe on her own yet. The pediatrician is hopeful she'll quickly be weaned from the respirator." She had to be or she wouldn't live, but he kept the knowledge to himself, hoping if he didn't speak about it, everything would be okay.

He sensed the other man's gaze on him.

"You love her."

EJ turned to look at the other man. Was he talking about Emily or the baby? Did it matter? "Yes. I want to marry Emily"--he swallowed hard and glanced back at the baby--"and raise Cadence as my own." He braced himself against the other man's objections.

Fabian let out a breath. "I'm glad she'll have a good father."

The quiet words brought EJ up short and he faced him. Fabian gave him a wry smile and shrugged his leather-clad shoulders. Long, dyed-black hair fell over his forehead, and he brushed it back with fingers tipped with dark polished nails. With his all black attire, he was the picture of the Goth music genre and the hard metal music it produced. Fabian cleared his throat and looked in at the baby. "My parents divorced when I was three. Mum and Dad had created this band--The Dark Fairy." He grinned at EJ, showing two slightly crooked front teeth. "Dad was Scottish and the name is a play on the original Gaelic meaning of McPhee. The band failed before it ever got off the ground. I named my band the same thing because it seemed to be a good name for a Goth pop band."

EJ had done some research on McPhee, and his story corroborated what he already knew of the man. His mother was killed in a car accident when he was four years old, and his father had remarried a half-dozen times before his death from a heart attack eighteen years ago when Fabian was nineteen years old.

"My father never wanted me around and sent me to one boarding school after another, going as long as two years before I'd even see him and whatever increasingly younger new wife he'd married." Fabian's voice took on a bitter note as he spoke. "I don't want that for my kid." He shook his head and lifted his shoulders in what might have been a shrug or an intake of breath. "That's why I didn't want any. I know I'm not father material."

EJ met Fabian's gaze and was taken aback by the pain shining in the man's dark blue eyes. Before he could speak, Fabian held out his hand to him. EJ shook it, surprised by the other man's strength.

"Take care of my daughter, Sheriff."

"I will."

Fabian headed down the hall, but before he turned the corner, he looked back at EJ. "I want you to adopt her. If Emily wants her to know I'm her biological father, fine." He shrugged and gave him that wry grin again. "If not, I know she will be in good hands."

* * * *

The last two months had flown by in spurts of worry and joy as baby Cadence agonizingly matured enough to leave the hospital. Emily sat in a padded rocking chair at the window of the room EJ had first given to her and held her baby to her breast. The bed she and EJ had first made love in had been taken down and stored in the attic. In its place was a beautiful white crib, a gift from her parents. After a moment of gazing on the perfectly rounded, red fuzzed head, she leaned her head back, closed her eyes, and enjoyed the strangely comforting pull of the baby's mouth on her nipple.

She'd never thought much about breastfeeding, but when the pediatrician and two nurses entered her room shortly after the birth and informed her mother's milk would be the best thing she could do for the baby, she didn't think twice about it. The nurses showed her how to pump her milk and instructed her on how to store it for when she was discharged. She'd brought the bags of frozen milk to the hospital on a daily basis for the tiny baby fighting for her life. Cadence flourished. By the time she was two weeks old, she or EJ could sit in the nursery and feed her from a bottle. It was on one of these visits a few weeks before she was released, Emily had asked about breastfeeding. The nurse had told her most likely Cadence wouldn't latch on, but they could try. With a lot of awkward coaxing, Cadence's tiny mouth latched on, and Emily had never experienced a closer bond to her daughter.

When Cadence let the nipple fall from her slack mouth, Emily glanced down and smiled at the sleeping baby. She shifted her to rest over her chest and gently patted her back until a loud un-baby-like belch emitted from the comatose bundle.

God, she hoped tonight would be the night she slept through till morning, or at least longer than her usual two-hour stretches. Despite the exhaustion, Emily was reluctant to put the baby down, but eventually, she stood and laid her daughter in the crib and tucked the soft blanket EJ's aunt had made around her still tiny body.

She looked one last time at the white crib and the baby within, before closing the door to stand ajar and heading across the hall. At the open door, she leaned against the doorframe and let the smile deepen at the scene before her. EJ sat on the edge of a twin-sized bed reading Dr. Seuss's *Cat in the Hat* to giggles from the squirming tow-headed boy in the bed. When Austin took notice of Emily, he scrambled out of bed and ran to her.

"Is sissy sleepin'?"

She reached down and swung the almost three-year-old up into her arms. "Yep. You are supposed to be sleeping, too, squirt." She blew a raspberry on the bare belly his scrunched up t-shirt revealed.

He let out a chorus of giggles and returned the favor with a big wet imitation on her cheek. "I'm not tired."

She fought the urge to wipe at the slobbery residue on her face. "Well, Daddy and I *are* tired."

"Ain't my fault sissy keeps you up," he said matter-of-factly, and she almost laughed.

EJ did chuckle, but ran a knuckle under his nose to stifle it when she frowned at him. He wasn't helping. "No, it isn't your fault, but it would be a big help if you did go to sleep."

He puckered his mouth as if in deep thought, before shrugged his little shoulders and flippantly, saying, "Okay, Mama. I'll go to sleep. If you sing the pretty song."

EJ and she had talked about what Austin would call her once he returned to Texas. At first, she was reluctant about him calling her any form of mother, but Austin had decided what to call her soon after arriving back home. Within two weeks, he was calling her mama. She'd tried to correct him, but EJ had assured her he'd already adopted her as his mommy and to tell him to do otherwise would only hurt him. Austin had never known Raquel, and pictures and half-remembered stories wouldn't ever fill the void left from not having a mother's love.

She hugged his warm solid body against her and kissed his forehead. He smelled of bubblegum-scented bath bubbles and little boy. If Austin had accepted her, she had more than fallen in love with the toddler as well. "Okay, I'll sing one song."

Despite Austin's antics, he yawned and laid his head on her shoulder. "Momma, sing to me."

EJ stood and smiled, moving to the side.

Emily laid Austin back into his rumpled bed and pulled the covers to his chin. She took EJ's place by his side, then sang the lullaby she'd written while sitting with Cadence in the hospital and hoped to record for her new record in the spring. *A Mother's Heart* was soft and soothing. By the time she reached the end, Austin's eyelids fluttered closed over his bright blue eyes. She hummed for a few more minutes until EJ gestured toward the door with a jerk of his chin.

At the door, she flipped off the light switch and gazed at the sleeping form on the bed as the fullness of the love she felt for her children expanded her heart to bursting.

EJ startled her when he took her hand and led her down the hall to their room.

To her parents' disappointment, she hadn't moved back to the Double K after leaving the hospital. EJ had asked her to move in with him, and she'd agreed. The Arrowhead Ranch was her home. He and their kids were her life. With a little bit of music mixed in.

He opened the door, and she drew in a breath as she stepped over the threshold. The room was aglow with dozens of candles, and on the dresser sat a tray holding two delicate fluted glasses. A moment of apprehension slithered through her when she picked a bottle out of a glass bowl filled with ice. A spurt of nervous laughter escaped as she set the non-alcoholic champagne bottle back in the makeshift chiller and turned toward him.

He smiled and reached past her to pick up the bottle, then poured the glasses half full. "Come over here." Gesturing with a cock of his head, he turned toward the bay window.

Distracted as she was upon entering the room by the candles and the *wine,* she hadn't noticed what was spread over the floor in front of the window. She rounded the side of the bed. "Is this a bear skin?"

He nodded and handed her one of the glasses. "Yeah. I found it in the attic when I stowed the bed. Come, sit."

With her heart pounding in her ears and all thought of her earlier exhaustion gone, she sat on the rug next to him. He'd opened the blinds and pulled back the curtains, to reveal the star-filled sky. The late September moon hung low in the eastern horizon, its big, silvery roundness filling the center of the window.

She pulled her attention away from the beauty of nature to look at EJ. Tiny beads of moisture glimmered over his forehead in the candlelight. The room was comfortable, but wasn't hot. Was he nervous?

He set his glass to the side on the hardwood floor. When he turned back to her, she looked around and set her glass on the floor, then shifted to face him. Once she settled again, he took both of her hands in his warm, work-roughened palms.

"Emily, I love you." His voice came out in a low sexy rumble, and her breath caught in her throat. "You and Cadence and Austin are the best things that ever happened to me."

He let go of her left hand and reached into his jeans pocket. She gasped when the pear-shaped diamond caught and splinted the candlelight.

"Oh, EJ." She met his beautiful pewter gaze and held her breath as he held the ring at the tip of her left ring finger.

"Will you marry me?"

A deep bone-affirming happiness settled over her, and she let out a sob of utter joy as she shifted her finger forward, allowing the ring to slip over her first joint. "Yes." She leaned in until her lips almost touched his, and before he could close the gap, she sang the hook of the song she'd written while sitting on the porch in July before all hell broke loose.

"Over blazing deserts or raging seas,
You are always there leading me,
No matter the chaos, you are my peace,
My love, my anchor, my forever guarantee."

"God, I love you," she whispered, then kissed him.

Be sure not to miss fellow Lyrical author Melissa Shirley's:

Breaking Hearts

Read on for a special sneak peek of the next book in the Storybook Lake series!

Learn more about Melissa Shirley
http://www.kensingtonbooks.com/author.aspx/31684

Chapter 1

Opening Statements

"All rise!"

Being on trial for my life taught me two things. One, when the bailiff says "all rise," everyone in the courtroom should immediately shut up and stand; two, the business end of being on trial and the tremors associated with it did not couple well with coffee drinking and silk blouses.

I blotted at my shirt while my lawyer leaned in close to advise me, yet again, of the possible outcomes of the case should I lose. Grace Wade turned to face me head-on and recommended I at least consider the prosecutions deal of life in prison with the possibility of parole in twenty-five years. Twenty-five years? I decided to gamble on a jury trial and a possible life sentence. Surely, at least one of the twelve people would realize I didn't kill Sean, no matter how badly I wanted to, and no matter how much unwavering gratitude, trial talk taboo, I harbored for the person who'd actually done the job.

The jurors filed into the courtroom, seven women between the ages of thirty and late sixties and five men from early twenties to late forties. A school teacher, bus driver, street sweeper, an accountant, landscaper, college student, and three food service professionals--translation: waiters and waitresses--a dog trainer, boutique owner, and a hairdresser, all had been chosen as my peers. Somehow, being accused of murder changed how I evaluated my peers, especially since I had no choice but to put my life in their hands.

Calvin Coolidge Connor, the prosecutor and apparent love child of Beetlejuice and Mr. Frodo--dark black hair, a slender waist, and a suit swallowing him almost whole--looked over at me with slits for eyes and a grim smirk on his lips. As green as any other small town thirty five-year-old prosecutor eager to make a name for himself, he probably jumped at the chance to take this case. He'd been an opportunist in high school, too, but as friends back then, I'd overlooked it. In this moment, with a gallery full of TV cameras, former friends, and reporters with pens poised to capture every detail, I hated him for it.

My attorney, the only lawyer I'd ever met, had been my best friend growing up, and though ten years had passed since we did more than make small talk on the phone, she took my case, no questions asked. Even though Grace had been career dormant as of late, I sat next to her not at all worried. She'd always been wrapped in some karmically blessed aura of greatness. At least, that's what I told myself in the morning before I dressed for trial.

She smoothed her skirt as we sat and waited for the prosecutor to begin his opening statement. At seventeen months older than me, Grace had movie star beauty. Along with her dramatic good looks, she capitalized on her porn star figure by wearing short, mostly respectable skirts, and blouses opened at the throat, thoroughly enhancing her pushed up C cups.

Without looking at me, checking her notes, or picking up a pen, she stared at the troll and waited. To anyone else, she appeared calm, poised for battle, but her fingers trembled as they sat idle against the table. A light sheen of sweat dotted her forehead and upper lip. We ignored the whirring of cameras, crinkling of papers, muffled coughs, hushed whispers in the court room, and most of our childhood friends on the witness list. For a former glory hound like Grace, ignoring it all said something.

As much as I'd come to love Storybook Lake over the last year, we weren't holding the trial at home. Storybook Lake would never let something so tainted as murder touch its cobblestoned, gas-lit streets. The proceedings had been transferred to neighboring Bloomington and my friends and former neighbors, all with ready-formed opinions as to my innocence or guilt, elbowed for space in the tiny courtroom.

Cal, whose grades in high school mirrored his initials, stood and walked to the center of the room, facing the jury, his back to me. While I understood he had a job to do, it irked me he'd been able to start without as much as a glance at the pile of notes on his table. Executing a perfect military turn in his too-shiny clown shoes, he took three paces toward the judge parallel to the jury, pulled in tight, turned a hard left and stalked to his original spot. He stopped abruptly, facing the twelve people instructed to hang on his every word.

"Good morning, ladies and gentlemen. My name is Calvin Connor and I represent you, the good people of the State of Illinois."

I nudged Grace and mouthed the words, "suck up." She shot me a glare and then went back to ignoring me.

"Storybook Lake, Illinois is an innocent little tourist town with a quiet character based on works of literary greatness. Its existence celebrates the lives of those who let us borrow their words to transport ourselves through whatever carefully woven life they have created in their pages. On June fourth, this woman"--he pointed at me without turning his head or body--"shattered the calm normally floating over the quiet little city. She lured her husband away from his home in California with the promise he would get to see the son she kidnapped."

I scanned the room for the Academy Award presenters and shrugged when no little gold statue or red carpet actress appeared.

Grace leaped to her feet. "Objection, Your Honor. Mrs. Turner had, and continues to have, sole custody of the child. There was no kidnapping involved and absolutely no evidence she lured her husband here. In fact, all evidence points otherwise." Grace turned to me, eyes wide and the hint of a smile on her lips.

The judge turned her attention to Cal. "Mr. Cooper?"

He simply lifted one shoulder, cocked his head toward it with an off-handed smile, offering no explanation.

"Sustained."

The judge shot him a dirty look.

He refocused on the jury and continued. "This woman, the defendant, is a cold, calculating killer who involved herself in a relationship with another man while still married to Sean Turner. She knew in order to be with the love of her life"--Air quotes?--"and raise her son with him, she needed to get rid of her husband. She had to make sure he didn't have the ability to interfere. So, what did she do? She took a knife and stabbed Sean Turner, not once, not twice, but seven times. And, in a matter of seconds, her burden of marriage disappeared."

He shook his head and clucked his tongue. "But then, Sean turner refused to die, to let her take his son away and live with another man. He refused to give up his hold on his wife and on life. She couldn't let him live, especially not now. Attempted murder? She would have lost her son, anyway. So, she ran to her purse, took out the gun she stole from her boyfriend, a former chief of police, and shot Mr. Turner in the face." He made a pistol with his fingers, flicked his arm out in aim. and shot me. "She lied to investigators, not once, but three times. She lied to her friends, her family, and to her son."

Grace rocket-launched out of her chair again. "Objection, Your Honor. May we approach?" Without waiting for an answer, she stomped to the front of the courtroom and stood, hands on hips, feet apart. Grace Wade, princess warrior, ready for battle.

After an animated discussion--her hands flailing, his head bobbing and the judge jerking her head back and forth ping pong style--she returned to her seat next to mine and picked up her pen. She scribbled, No worries. I got this.

I aspired to worried.

The judge glanced at Cal, then the jury. "The objection is sustained. Ladies and gentleman, there is no evidence the gun used to shoot Mr. Turner was, in fact, the gun belonging to Simon Hunter." Cal received his second stink-eye from the judge in a matter of minutes. "Proceed, Mr. Connor."

"The point isn't who this defendant lied to or whose gun she used, or why Sean Turner turned up in Illinois. The point is she lied and she lied a lot. She left Mr. Turner in his hotel room bleeding to death."

Nope. By the time I arrived, he'd been stabbed and shot and died alone. The way I always knew he would.

"The relationship between the defendant and Mr. Turner was born in the back of a limousine where the defendant conceived the couple's child. After trying unsuccessfully to dupe Keaton Shaw into believing the child belonged to him, a DNA test proved her a liar. Another lie in her long list. With no other choice after being chased out of Storybook Lake in shame, she sought out Sean Turner and married him, then quit her job."

I hadn't quit my job. My job didn't require a desk or an office, just a pen and piece of paper. I designed kids' clothes for a living.

"Then she moved to California to be with her husband. After a few thousand arguments over money, she left the marital home, taking the child with her. When she returned over the Christmas holiday, she visited Storybook Lake with her husband, and while they were there, together, as a couple, she flaunted her desire to be with Mr. Hunter in Sean Turner's face."

We had been fighting over my money and the way Sean spent it in big fat wads, but the tone of Cal's voice turned the greed around on me. And, for his information, during the trip in question, Sean found me talking to Simon for the sum total of one minute, hauled me back to the hotel, and hit me with such force my eyes rolled back. I thought he'd literally broken my face. The next morning, he'd cried like a baby, said he couldn't stand the thought of losing me. I went home with him because he'd been sorry and because he promised to start over with me and make a life with me and Kieran. Plus, Simon went to the New Year's party with Kelly Devlin, the big shot magazine writer he'd broken up with me to date.

"Mr. Turner, by this defendant's own admission, cried, begged, and pleaded for her to return to him so he could share in the life of their child. Reluctantly, by another of her own admissions, she returned home to Mr. Turner where the real fighting began."

Rage at the injustice behind Cal's half-truths welled up inside me. Grace covered my fingers with her own, squeezing hard, probably to stop the drumming against the table top. The fighting started because Sean slept with every stripper in his employ, as well as some who worked for other clubs. Jeez! Where was a tiny-headed voodoo doll when I needed one?

"By the time she finished with him, Sean Turner couldn't wait for Danielle to leave, but he wanted his son. Within hours of her leaving, he filed papers for custody of his child."

Sean had used custody as leverage to lure me back. I resisted the urge to roll my eyes. Grace had been forthright about how I should behave, and eye rolling topped the no-no list.

"But did this defendant cooperate after the police found the body? Did she ever tell them she had, in fact, been in Mr. Turner's hotel room? No. Did she tell them she stalked him to the hotel, fought with him? No. Instead, she pretended she'd had no contact with him since she'd taken their son and run home to Storybook Lake months earlier." He shook his head and his pacing in front of the jury continued.

"When investigators discovered otherwise, her story changed again, tailored to fit the evidence. She finally concocted this story of abuse toward not only her, but the child. She, in her desperation to stay out of jail, involved their four-year-old son in her web of lies." He stared down most of the time, presumably to make sure his clown shoes didn't catch on one another and cause him to topple head over feet. "Danielle Turner is the worst kind of predator. She uses her beauty"--he stabbed a bony finger through the air in my direction and gazed up at the jury--"to snare men into her web of lies."

His words curdled my blood.

"She used her over-average intelligence to try to outwit cops and investigators. And she used her son as a weapon to get her way. In this case, to get her way she had to kill Mr. Turner. Otherwise, she couldn't embark on her new life with Simon Hunter. In a town which celebrates its fiction, don't lump her in with the likes of Shakespeare, Mark Twain, or even Dr. Seuss. Her fiction is as unbelievable as the evidence will prove it to be." With a smirk, he raised one eyebrow at Grace and went back to his chair, needing a copy of the yellow pages on his seat to properly see over the top of his table. Without it, he seemed to have tucked himself almost underneath the smooth, flat surface holding the mountain of notes and binders on the case.

Grace stood and smoothed her skirt. "Mr. Connor." She shook her head, long, blond hair swinging along her back, soft curls dancing. "Shame on you."

"Your Honor." Calvin shoved his legs against the fabric of his cushioned chair, shooting it backward into the short wall dividing us from the gallery. The clatter echoed throughout the high-ceilinged room. "Ms. Wade needs to speak to the jury, not the prosecutor."

The judge smiled at Grace. "Miss Wade, you know better."

Grace nodded, her lips pursing as she tried to wipe the smile from her face. "Yes, Your Honor." She turned back to the jury and introduced herself, then began. "Mrs. Turner didn't lure her husband to Storybook Lake. She didn't want him anywhere near Storybook Lake or her son. Since the day of their wedding, Sean tortured Danielle, beating her and later Kieran. There is irrefutable evidence to prove it."

She turned to Cal, with another quick shake of her head as though reprimanding him for his lie. "As soon as the private detective Sean Turner hired to hunt Danielle found her, bad, scary, dangerous things started to happen. He had her home vandalized, then broken into. She received countless texts on numerous cell phones indicating Sean knew exactly where to find her and exactly how she spent her days. The week he died, Sean bought a plane ticket and flew to Storybook Lake to step up his efforts to intimidate my client, her friends, and her family. The evidence will show you Danielle did not kill Mr. Turner.

"Instead you'll see how Sean Turner taunted her, threatened her life repeatedly, not only over the last week of his life, but during the entire course of their relationship. What the evidence will not show you is that she had a single thing to do with his murder. The prosecutor has no murder weapon, no eye witness, not a single, tangible thing to prove Danielle had anything to do with Sean's murder. She admitted to seeing him. She admitted to being in his hotel room, but no matter how hard they tried, they couldn't shake her story about what happened after she got there."

She paused for a moment, her eyes pivoting from me to the jury. "You are going to hear things about Sean Turner which are going to make it seem as though he's the one on trial, about his behavior, his job, and his sex life. Make no mistake. We're not trying to smear Sean Turner's name, but this is all information you need to walk into the jury room with a full picture of the events leading up to the night Danielle left her husband and returned home to the safety of Storybook Lake.

"Danielle had the most to lose and nothing to gain by Sean Turner's death. When he died, she inherited an almost bankrupt strip club and a pile of debt he ran up in the months since she left. She had an army of friends surrounding her to keep her safe from Sean and his henchmen. The fact is, many, many people had a reason to want Sean dead. Danielle didn't kill him, and Mr. Cooper cannot prove otherwise."

Grace smiled once more at the jury, then came to sit beside me as Calvin stood. "Your Honor," he said, with enough glee in his voice I imagined him about to spring into cartwheels. "I call Mr. Keaton Shaw."

Ugh. Keaton's debt to me had been repaid, and no matter what he said about forgiving me, I had no idea what he would say or do on the stand. He raised his right hand, swore to tell the truth, and took his seat to the left of the judge. After he stated his name for the record, he shot me a half smile. I hoped against all other hope it was a good sign.

When he tightened his tie, adjusted his jacket, then pointed a straight-forward gaze at the jury, several of the female jurors sat up straighter. His beauty inspired the same reaction wherever he went.

"Mr. Shaw." Calvin walked from his seat to the podium, almost wringing his hands together in evil merriment. This had to be his nerd dream. He had the captain of every sports team in our graduating class sitting in front of him testifying against the homecoming queen. It played out like an after school special gone wrong. "How do you know Mrs. Turner?"

Keaton's eyebrows moved toward the center of his forehead as though he'd never heard a question more stupid. "We all grew up together." His tone clearly indicated he included Calvin in the group.

Calvin chuckled. "Right. We did."

Though I'm sure Cal remembered growing up outside their circle a little differently than Keaton remembered growing up surrounded by Gatlin, Joss, Simon, Kelly, and Luke.

"Growing up, how well did you get to know Mrs. Turner?"

Keaton smiled. "We were friends, then we dated in high school. After high school we lived together for a while."

"And when you were living together, was it while you were still married?"

Uh-oh.

"I was in the process of getting divorced."

"But you were still married?" Cal's question left Keaton no room to wiggle out of the answer.

"Yes." He ground out the word as one eyebrow cocked on his forehead, daring Cal to take it further.

A bubble of anger formed in the pit of my stomach as Calvin asked, "And your divorce stemmed from your involvement with Mrs. Turner?"

Oh, good Lord. I nudged Grace. Object, dammit. She'd never been good at hearing my mind messages, so I kicked her shin. She whirled to look at me and tilted her head. "Stop."

"My wife thought I was having an affair." Explain, explain, explain. I hoped Keaton had the gift of telepathy Grace did not. Unfortunately, he remained sitting, hands clasped in his lap, waiting for the next question.

Calvin continued grinding his ugly little axe to a razor sharp point. "During the time you lived with Mrs. Turner, did either of you use drugs or alcohol?"

"Yes." Keaton looked at me and frowned.

"Both of you?"

"We didn't do drugs."

I closed my eyes as memories of those days washed over me…dim, alcohol-fogged memories.

"And during your time away, Mrs. Turner became pregnant?"

I wanted to smack Cal's self-satisfied smile right off his smarmy, thin lips. If eye rolling topped Grace's no-no list, I had to assume smacking the prosecutor was off-limits, but the desire itched inside my palm.

"Yes."

"And she let you believe the child belonged to you for how long?"

"She didn't do it on purpose. We lived together like couples live together."

I guessed that was his way of saying we'd had some sex. Knowing Joss had a seat a few rows behind me, I couldn't decide if his lie helped or hurt either of us.

"He could have been mine." Keaton frowned.

Calvin peered up at the judge. "Your Honor, the witness is non-responsive."

The judge glared back at Calvin. "And your question was leading. Rephrase." She shot a lifted brow look at Grace.

"How long did Mrs. Turner let you believe you'd fathered her child?"

Grace stood up. "Objection. Relevance and foundation."

The judge looked at Grace, a half smile crooking her lips. "Sustained."

Calvin clarified the details. When had we lived together and where? How long after we began living together did I become pregnant? How long after I told him did I have the baby?

"And how long before you discovered he belonged to someone else?"

Grace stood again. "Objection, relevance."

"Your honor, it goes to her motive for seeking out Mr. Turner in the first place."

Grace almost popped her hip out of place coming around the desk, and for a split second, I thought she might wrap her hands around his neck instead of punching them against her waist. "Your Honor, we believed Mr. Shaw was going to be called because he was a first responder to the scene."

"She can't tell me what to ask my witness." Calvin's voice climbed to a child-like whine.

The judge cocked her head. "Approach, please." They walked to the front of the courtroom, and I sat back in my chair, remembering.

www.ingramcontent.com/pod-product-compliance
Lightning Source LLC
Chambersburg PA
CBHW050753250626
47155CB00005B/2046